La

Donated by
Friends
of the
Del Webb Library

MID-AIR

Also by Alicia D. Williams

Genesis Begins Again

Jump at the Sun

The Talk

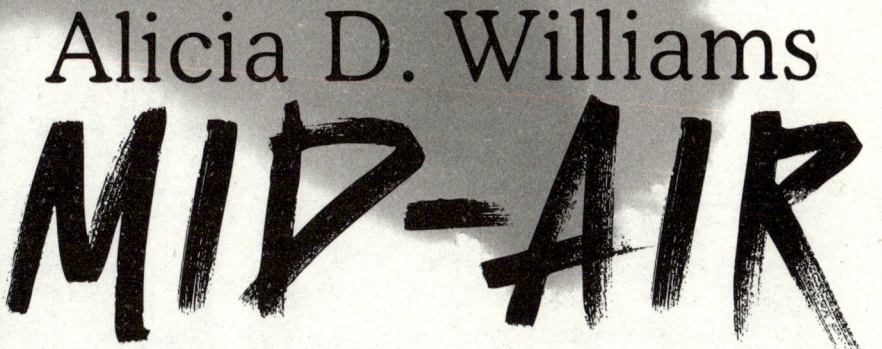

Alicia D. Williams
MID-AIR

Illustrated by Danica Novgorodoff

A CAITLYN DLOUHY BOOK

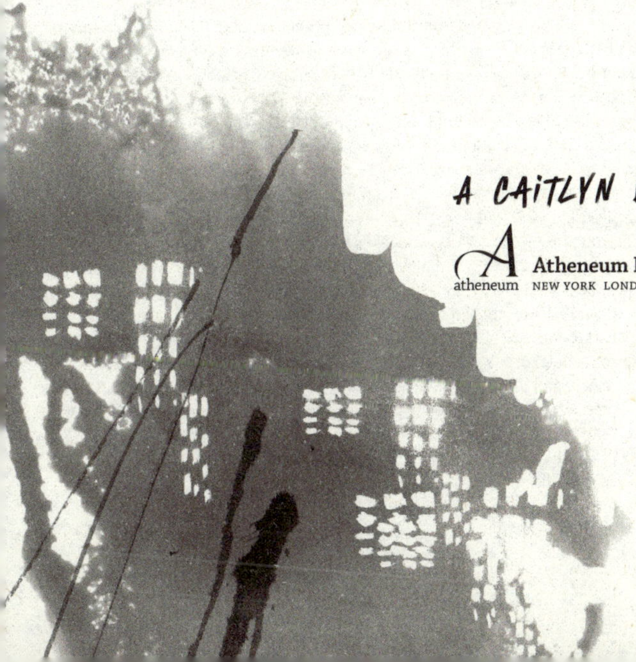

Atheneum Books for Young Readers
NEW YORK   LONDON   TORONTO   SYDNEY   NEW DELHI

atheneum

ATHENEUM BOOKS FOR YOUNG READERS · An imprint of Simon & Schuster Children's Publishing Division · 1230 Avenue of the Americas, New York, New York 10020 · This book is a work of fiction. Any references to historical events, real people, or real places are used fictitiously. Other names, characters, places, and events are products of the author's imagination, and any resemblance to actual events or places or persons, living or dead, is entirely coincidental. · Text © 2024 by Alicia D. Williams · Jacket illustration © 2024 by Daniel Egnéus · Jacket design by Debra Sfetsios-Conover · Interior illustration © 2024 by Danica Novgorodoff · All rights reserved, including the right of reproduction in whole or in part in any form. · ATHENEUM BOOKS FOR YOUNG READERS is a registered trademark of Simon & Schuster, LLC. Atheneum logo is a trademark of Simon & Schuster, LLC. · Simon & Schuster: Celebrating 100 Years of Publishing in 2024 · For information about special discounts for bulk purchases, please contact Simon & Schuster Special Sales at 1-866-506-1949 or business@simonandschuster.com. · The Simon & Schuster Speakers Bureau can bring authors to your live event. For more information or to book an event, contact the Simon & Schuster Speakers Bureau at 1-866-248-3049 or visit our website at www.simonspeakers.com. · The text for this book was set in Cooper Lt BT. · The illustrations for this book were rendered in ink and watercolor. · Manufactured in the United States of America · 0324 BVG · First Edition · 10 9 8 7 6 5 4 3 2 1 · Library of Congress Cataloging-in-Publication Data · Names: Williams, Alicia D., 1970– author. | Danica Novgorodoff, illustrator. · Title: Mid-air / by Alicia D. Williams ; illustrated by Danica Novgorodoff. · Description: First edition. | New York : Atheneum Books for Young Readers, 2024. | "A Caitlyn Dlouhy Book." | Audience: Ages 10 up. | Audience: Grades 7–9. | Summary: Thirteen-year-old Isaiah grapples with the loss of his best friend as he strives to fit into a world that expects him to toughen up, which leads him on an exploration of identity and vulnerability. · Identifiers: LCCN 2023029800 (print) | LCCN 2023029801 (ebook) | ISBN 9781481465830 (hardcover) | ISBN 9781481465854 (ebook) · Subjects: CYAC: Novels in verse. | Grief—Fiction. | Identity—Fiction. | African Americans—Fiction. | BISAC: JUVENILE FICTION / People & Places / United States / African American & Black | JUVENILE FICTION / Social Themes / Self-Esteem & Self-Reliance | LCGFT: Novels in verse. · Classification: LCC PZ7.5.W535 Mi 2024 (print) | LCC PZ7.5.W535 (ebook) | DDC [Fic]—dc23 · LC record available at https://lccn.loc.gov/2023029800 · LC ebook record available at https://lccn.loc.gov/2023029801

FOR ELIJAH.

AND FOR ANYONE WHO HAS HIDDEN A PART OF THEMSELVES, THIS IS FOR YOU, MY DEARS. BE BOLD AND BRAVE. AND MOST OF ALL, BE AUTHENTICALLY YOU.

Bet

Swear this word is gon' get us killed, yo.

All three of us stand in front of the HUGEST
dirt mound we've ever seen.
Not just dirt. Nah. A beast of
rubble, bricks, stones, plywood, & a bunch of
heck if I knows hidden throughout like booby traps.
Like the city knocked down a whole building &
the demolition team up & quit. Left it all in a heap.

Told you. Drew cheeses like he one-upped us.
He ain't tell us.
For the thirty-minute hike it took to get here—
Drew. Did. Not. Tell. Us. *This.*

An hour ago, Drew bragged how he & his old squad
used to race bikes down a hill. Talking about
how dudes wiped out. But not him.
Me & Darius got tired of his yapping,
so we bet Drew we could do it too.

I figured conquering a li'l hill would get him
off my back about choking—
or what my English teacher calls *reevaulating*—
the last few dares.

But dang, wasn't picturing no bootleg Mount Kilimanjaro.
Got us standing around with thirty other kids
plotting & planning how to conquer this thing.

What is that, like, two stories? I say.
    Darius, to my right, answers, *Nah, more like a*
    glorious three.

Drew, to my left, jaws, *Yo, it's not that bad.*
    Not that bad? I gawk at him. *Dude?*
    We looking at the same thing?
He laughs like I'm kidding. I'm not kidding.

Sure, you got this? Drew asks for the hundredth time.
Darius turns to me. *Isaiah, you got this, right?*
Yeah. I swallow hard. *I got it.*
Drew thrusts out his hand. *Aight. Bet.*

Mannn, Dude always wanna bet somebody.
He don't care about the gang of boys standing around
rubbing wounds & fighting to get next
while taking bets on each rider's life. On they *life!*

Yo, for real, this ain't a jumping-off-my-garage's-roof
ankle-straining bet.
Or a skateboard-down-city-hall's-handrail
wrist-fracturing bet.
Naw,   this   is   a   legit
leg-breaking back-buckling better-not-cry bet.
Still, I shove out my hand. *Bet.*

A kid now at the top straddles his wheels.
Hoots & hollers whoop the air. Darius nudges me,
I nudge him, & whoa, off bro goes.

His arms flap with each bump hit & pothole dip—
He ain't gon' make it!
He twists left. Grips too tight—
Loosen up, man! Loosen up!
He brakes & swerves & wobbles—
Stay on the path! Yo, stay on the path!
He veers right, hits a brick, skyrockets ten feet, & *bam—*
    Ummph!

Dirt shifts. Rocks scatter.
We watch. We wait. & *whoa—*
bro's got a bloody nose.
He swipes his arm across his face & pops up—
Yo, you see that! Almost made it this time!
    He ain't almost make it.

Drew rubs his hands together like he's expecting big bucks.
He looks to Darius, then me, & grins.
Eenie meenie miney mo, which one of y'all is first to go?

Who's First?

Gray clouds hover above like
it's gonna rain any minute.   Hopefully.
Bro's nose is bleeding.
A lot.   Unfortunately.

Darius unzips his puffer jacket.
Throws it to the ground.
Me. I got next.

Ahh dang, I was gon' go, I say, fast.
Drew smirks. *Yeah, right.*

Darius pushes his BMX up the hill.
Seems like it takes forever to get to the top.
Finally, there, he mounts his bike & studies the path.

His shoulders rise & fall.
      I chew the side of my mouth.
He braces one foot on a pedal.
      I shove my jacket sleeves up.
He angles forward.
      I do too.

In three, two, one—he blasts off.
Shoots down the mountain super-fast!
Doubles over like a jockey.
Hands steer left & right, feet pedal & brake.
We're yelling & jumping & pumping fists in the air
when Darius's front tire grazes a cement block &—
Ahhhhhhhhhh!—
he soars like Miles Morales—
hits the ground, tumbling tumbling—
Drew & I run over. *Hey, you okay?*

Darius is splat-flat on his back, spread out like a starfish.
Yo, that was bananas! Isaiah, bruh, you gotta do it.

Gotta? That mountain is a death trap. *A death trap!*
Bleeding-nose boy pinches his nostrils,
another cradles his elbow, & Darius is laid out!

I know, I know I gotta—*gonna* do it—because
part of me imagines me crushing it too.
Imagines them clapping me on my back too.
Yeah. That happening. To me. For real. For once.

I hold out my hand.
Darius grabs, pulls up. *That's gotta be GOAT-tier
Guinness World Record–breaking.*

Drew points to the side of Darius's dome.
That knot growing on yo' head'll break a record.

Darius rubs it.
Then he spots his busted tire. *Dag.*

Darius had us popping wheelies the whole way here.
Talking about how it's our *next* world record. But
how's he gon' pop if he can't even ride? *What you gonna do?*

Darius pokes the tire. *Get it fixed. Fast.*

Just then, it starts to sprinkle. A kid rushes up the hill.
We wait for me to get next. Drew & Darius don't say it,
but they're expecting me to—

Choke.

Okay, so yeah, I
choked at the skate park.
Choked on top of the garage.
Choked when backflipping off a tree.
Doesn't mean I'mma flake this time.
I peep the mountain again.
Please, Isaiah, don't flake.

The kid ahead of me takes a nosedive. Yikes!
My turn.

You got this, Drew says, with a chin raise.
Aye, be like water. Darius reaches out & we
front hand slap, back hand slap, dap, dap, palm clasp.

The sprinkle turns to drizzle.
The narrow path is worn slick from tires & blood
of other kids trying to be king.
Even slicker now from the rain.

I slip. Almost fall.
Calls of *Hurry up!* from boys I don't know.
Be like water! from Darius who I do.

The rain keeps drizzling, the ground gets slicker,
my feet keep slipping, & I keep pushing until . . .
I make it to the top. The tip tip top!
Yo, it takes all my might not to beat my chest
King Kong style & shout, *I did it! I climbed the beast!*

I hop on my bike. Study the path like Darius did.
But dag, the slope seems steep. Like, STEEP steep.
My mind flashes to Darius & the other kids wiping out.
To the bloody nose & the slippery path.
To the hidden traps & my almost fall.
To me teetering over the edge of my garage's roof.
To—*Chill,* I tell myself. *Be like water.*

I wanna be like water. I really do.
Wanna ride down & come up laughing even if I flop.
Wanna have my boys finally give me props.
But no matter how long I stand here psyching myself—
no matter the next boy is rushing me to get going—
no matter that a bet was made. Today ain't that day &
I
    can't
        do it.

My fingers find my coat pocket & pull out my beanie.
I put it on till it nearly covers my eyes &
I
       slink
               down.

Kids call me weak. Punk. Worse.
My brain pesters me with jokes
Darius & Drew could crack.

I don't see the hole that traps my foot,
makes me trip & Humpty-Dumpty down down down.
I lie there. Wait for this monster to swallow me,
drag me deep into its belly. Yeah, dramatic, I know.
But rather that than face them.

Darius grabs my bike. *Dude, you good?*
Mud slinks down the side of my face like slime.
My leg throbs. *Yeah.*

What happened? You almost had it, Drew says.
Before I can respond, he gives me his hand, yanks me up.
Just kidding. But aye, why you ain't use your Spidey webs?

I shake the dizzies out my head.
What?

Your Spidey webs. He flicks up his wrist.
You know, to break yo' fall.

You stupid, I say, laughing for the first time since we got here. I mean, his joke *is* kinda funny.

Darius clamps our shoulders. *Y'all owe me.*
We coming back and both y'all riding. Bet?

Bet, says Drew.
Yeah, I say. *Bet.*

But for real, your boy is almost fresh outta bets.

Our Origin Story

Me & Darius been boys since
the first day of robotics camp.
The only two out of twenty
with faces penny brown.
The only two out of twenty
left standing after partner picking.

Wanna work together? he asked, like
it was a choice. For either of us.

In between connecting wires to
batteries to further connect to
motors & building a Raspberry Pi,
we shot off questions like—

You watch WWE?
Yeah. You play Minecraft?
Heck yeah, you skate?
Sometimes. You like comics?
All over 'em. Ever break a world record?

Then Came Drew

It was last April, seventh grade, in the schoolyard
at the concrete slab we hijacked from
the magic tarot-reading girls & which is now known
as *the* Four Square Corner, when this new kid,
with a scrunched-up face, stood in line. None of us
said nothing to him. He said nothing to us. Yet, he stood.

Marcus got out, New Kid stepped in across from
Darius, next to Randy, diagonal from me.
He eyed us. We eyed him. Sizing.
Ready? said Darius.
Three heads nodded. The ball started moving.

We played so long, wet dripped down our faces.
We played so hard, our hair follicles sweated.

Kids, some, then more, surrounded us; eyes followed
the ball as hands smacked it forward & sideways.
We were all on some superhero-save-the-world-type
focus. Bending air, earth, & water. The rise & fall of
*ohhh*s & *ooo*s played like a soundtrack.

New Kid couldn't get me or Darius out.
We couldn't get him.
We matched like this till break ended.

New Kid stuffed his hands into his pockets.
Mean mug face on one hundred.
Darius gave dap. *What's your name?*
He gave dap back. *Drew.*
Darius bounced the ball. *Cool, cool. You got game.*
Drew took the ball, dribbled. *Got more than that.*
I stuck out my fist. *I'm Isaiah.*
And *I'm Darius,* said Darius. *You can roll with us.*

Every day, at our lockers, during lunch, at the
Four Square Corner, we threw out questions like—
You played this at your old school?
Drew: *Not really. Y'all ball?*
Sometimes. You skate?
Drew: *Naw, but I'm nice with a bike. You watch MMA?*
Nah. Ever break a world record?

Just like that, Drew's Detroit hard upgraded me &
Darius's suburban geek.
Just like that, we hung out after school. Weekends too. &
pretty much ever since,
      when you see Darius
                      you see Drew
                                    you see me.

Plant Life

One thing to know about a plant is
the type of light it needs.

For example, fiddle-leafs & jades
need direct light to best grow.
But Chinese money plants & peace lilies
want low, indirect light to thrive.

Yeah, okay, your boy knows a li'l
something something about our green friends.

That's because of my mom. She's a plant stylist.
People hire her to style their spaces with plants in
designer pots. & I'm her assistant. Yes, a plant assistant.
Don't trip. It's a job. Mom pays me.

But for real, Mom's never met a plant she didn't want.

We got philodendrons & snake plants in corners.
Split-leaf philodendrons & monsteras at the base of stairs.
Golden pothos & string of pearls hang from the ceiling.

Cactus here, baby rubber plants there—
swear she's got plants everywhere.

& right now, my fingers gently hold the stem of
a white-dotted green leaf cast iron plant I'm propagating.

So, check it, propagation is
when you take small cuttings from a plant &
put them in water or soil to make a whole new plant.
Cool, right? Anyway . . .

AC/DC blasts in the background 'cause
these plants roll with rock. I sing—
but not to the cast iron; let's not make this weird, yo—
& tuck stems into tiny pots of soil as I picture a T-shirt
I wanna buy.

But whoa, not just any T-shirt.
Not the mass-printed ones sold everywhere
that everybody wears.
Not the retro new-school tees made to look
old-school either.
Naw, a—

1986   Aerosmith   Aero Force One Tour tee.

Yo, I got the illest vintage rock band tee collection going on.
Mostly classic right now. Own seven so far.
Def Leppard, 1988.   Guns N' Roses, 1989.
Journey, 2016.   Nirvana, 1999.
Van Halen, 1993.   Metallica, 1980.

& I still nerd out over my first one.
Found it at a flea market
Mom dragged me to when I was ten.
She was at a table picking through
Mexican flowerpots. I was at another
sifting through Teenage Mutant Ninja Turtle tees
when my hands landed on a black shirt
with gold letters & a woman with wings—
Led. Freaking. Zeppelin.
The band that made
the iconic—the *iconic!*—

"Immigrant Song"

So, I was sitting in the theater, watching *Thor: Ragnarök*.
Popcorn salty. Movie's fire. Soundtrack bangs.
Song comes on. Fast-rocking guitar blares.
Then a scream—
AHHHHHH-AH!!!
Thor burst onscreen, cape flying, hammer mid-air—
AHHHHHH-AH!!!
It wasn't Thor or his hammer that hooked me.
It was Led Zeppelin's
thunderously loud, absurdly wild,
come and get some—
AHHHHHH-AH!!!
Those dudes scream
on full blast in all CAPS, plus triple exclamation marks.
Don't care who likes it or not.
Don't care if you like *them* or not.
AHHHHHH-AH!!!
Yo,
that roar opened the door
to the Isaiah
I want to be.

Plant Life, Cont'd

Mom asks if I want to make an extra twenty dollars.
She tosses back her brown curly hair that hangs
past her shoulders like string of pearls succulents
& tells me the task: repot the bird-of-paradise.

I walk around the bird. Lift the base of the tree.
Grunt & groan cause the plant's kinda heavy.
Picture that sweet Aerosmith tee in my hands,
knowing I need at least twenty-five to add to
the one hundred to buy it. *This is a biggie.*
How about thirty?

Deal. She agrees a little too fast, leaving me wondering
if I should've asked for more.

But I shrug it off because what Mom doesn't know is
I'd do this work for free.

Hypes

Darius & Drew are at my door with boards in hand
talking about *We gotta go. Come on! Hurry up!*
Where? I ask, praying not back to that mountain.

Klean Streak Sneaks, they say at the same time.
    Bro, adds Drew, *hypes dropped.*
Exclusives, says Darius.
    The Nike Air Jordan 1—
High 1985!
    Ohhh. Riiight, I say.

We skate down side streets,
    up main streets,
slip between cars,
    hop curbs,
around corners,
    all the way
to where colorful stores are lined
    side by side like LEGO blocks.

Cupcakes Galore . . . Tony's Pizza . . . Amelia's Coffee . . .
Fluff Stuff Pet Shop . . . Bob's Hardware—

Yooooo, they giving away Jays? I joke.
A line of sneakerheads, already a block long,
wait to buy kicks to collect, wear, or resell.

A man at the door admits only a few people at a time.
We fall in line behind two older guys.
Their heads stay down, eyes focus on phones.
Nobody talks to nobody as we slowly snail forward.

Darius rubs the knot on his head from the other day &
starts up about the mountain. *Thinking we should add it
to our list. Racing down it a couple times without wiping
out gotta break a world record, right?*

Drew nods. *Gotta.*
   I nod too, but trust, I'm good with never going back.
Just say when and we in, Drew says. *We swore, right, I?*
   Yep, I mumble, & scuff a cigarette butt,
    grind it into the ground.

We shuffle ahead a few more feet.

   Hey, I say. *Who's buying sneaks?*
Darius wipes his nose. *We just gon' try 'em on.*
   I blow into my hands. *Try them on?*
Yeah, blurts Drew. *Hots cost at least $250. Who got that?*
   I dig out my gloves. *So we roll all the way here
   just to try on kicks?*
They look at me like I'm sus. Like *I'm* sus.

The smell of cinnamon floats from the bakery.
My stomach rumbles.
We roll here—in the cold—with no money.

Darius smirks. *Just wanna see how fresh I look standing in Jays.*
He faces his reflection in the store window, smooths over his
cornrows. *But your boy can't get no fresher.*

After an hour—*an hour!*—the man waves us in.
A whoosh of heat thaws my cheeks as we file straight
to a wall full of Jordans. Drew points to a style, gives
the salesclerk his size, Darius follows suit, & I do too.

Check this out. Drew picks up a display.
White soles. Red bottoms. Black swoop. Black strings.
Can't tell me these ain't sick.

Darius raises high a green & white shoe. *I present to you . . .
the Holy Grails.* He turns the sneak this way & that
until another clerk asks us not to touch them.
We need to keep them clean, he explains.

Our guy comes back with three boxes stacked
in his arms. Drew cheeses so hard his eyes disappear.

Drew delicately unwraps the left & right shoes & sniffs.
Mmm, fresh leather. He carefully eases a foot into each.
Soon as he ties the laces, he's in the mirror flexing.
Darius is up a second later, one leg in front of the other,

posing. I stuff my feet fast into the sneaks, stick my
foot into the frame, & get my top model on too.

The line outside stretches longer & longer. Still, we try
on pair after pair. The white, black, & grays. Straight
black & reds. White & blue, with black swoops. Until Drew
snaps his fingers. *Aye, can we try on—*

Hey. The clerk stops, his forehead bulleted with sweat.
You all buying or trying?

Drew slips the Jays back into the box & grins.
Yo, we just wanna be like Mike, that's all.

Be like Mike?
It takes two seconds for his words to land before
we're cracking up & they're putting us out with
stomachs rumbling from the smell of cinnamon buns
without a dollar in our pockets to buy a bite to share.

Sold

No no no no no.
Gone. It's gone!
I refresh the site hoping, just hoping
the *items in cart* = 0 box is wrong.
But naw, it's gone.
The dopest 1986 Aerosmith Aero Force One tour tee
with the red AEROSMITH above a big blue seal
with an eagle in the middle rocking old-school headphones
with gold stars & gold-to-silver-ombre
AERO FORCE ONE lettering—

Sold.

Thin Blood

It snows all morning. Mom makes me shovel.
Dad usually does it. But he's off in Benin.
Or is it Belize? Somewhere with a *B*.

Was home in February. Brought Mom an
African milk tree & chocolate-covered strawberries
for Valentine's. Mom went wilder over the plant
than the strawberries.

Ever since he started that job last year, he's hardly home.
But sends packages like Santa Claus.

        Weaved baskets, braided bracelets, vintage dolls,
        tribal art, carved bowls, teas & chocolates,
        colored pencils, squid chips from Thailand,
        socks & chopsticks from South Korea,
        stuff & stuff & stuff.

        His laptop is full of photos of orphaned koala bears
        dreaming of homes before the forests burned,
        tuskless elephants robbed of ivory by poachers,
        the women soldiers sworn to protect them, &

      newly discovered descendants of an extinct tortoise
                      on the Galápagos Islands.
              All for *National Geographic* magazine.

Mom wraps a scarf around my neck.
I tell her I don't need all that, but
she tells me I've got thin blood.

I say, *What the heck is thin blood?*
She says, *Just as it sounds. Not thick enough to keep you warm.*
Says that's why I can't handle the cold.

Pretty sure she made that up.
But I'm not about to voice that
'cause I got my eye on another Aerosmith shirt—
a 1993 concert tee—
that immediately after this snow shoveling
will be bought
by me.

Cocoa in the Closet

It takes three hours to finish. *Three hours!*
My fingers are stiff. My back is broke.
All I wanna do is lie down.

But Mom has hot cocoa waiting for me.
I'm about to complain. Can't be sitting around
drinking cocoa like some kid. But after one sip,
my lips are zipped. Because, come on, it's cocoa.

Me & my drink escape into my closet
sidestep sneaks spread on the floor like spilt Cheerios &
a box of comics me & Darius read hundreds of times

to the back, where there's a basket of clothes I want to
but won't dare wear anywhere except in here,
then change into a burning skull tee, ripped black jeans,
& a leather spiked fingerless glove.

In here, I'm not wannabe-white-boy-rock-star Black.
That's what Randy & Marcus called me
when I admitted to liking rock.

Had everybody calling me
White Boy & Metal Head.
Had everybody, except Darius.

So I swore off rock. Switched to rap . . .
except in here, where it's just me & the *da-da-da-daah*—
                Gawds of Rock!—
  AC/DC, Led Zeppelin, Aerosmith, Queen, KISS, Metallica,
            Kansas, Jimi Hendrix, & Prince—
taped to all the walls in my closet.
Got some hard-core punk plus funk rockers too.
    Bad Brains, Fishbone, Death, Meet Me @ the Altar,
           Panic! at the Disco . . .

I start a playlist from my phone,
jam out to the first song—the OBGMs—
when my cell dings.

You In or What?

Drew: *Meeting up to play fball in the field. Y'all in?*
Darius: *I'm down what about you I?*
I take a sip of cocoa.
My head bops to "Torpedo."
Hmmm . . . bet Randy & Marcus'll be there.
They used to, most times still do, dog everybody.
But once you're in with them, you're in.
       Buuuuuuuuut—
Last time I played,
the football slipped from my hands
two too many times.
They clowned me.
Wouldn't throw me the ball
the rest of the game.

I take another sip of cocoa.
Hmmm . . . football in the snow with Marcus & Randy.
I type back *Can't. Mom's working me.*

I mean, come on, I've got thin blood. *Thin blood!*

Darius Is Back At It

At lunch, Darius goes on & on about his fixed bike &
how he's been doing push-ups. He flexes his bicep.
*My arms are John Cena attitude adjustment strong.
Don't believe me? Feel.*

Drew pushes his arm away. *Bruh, we believe you.*
    Yeah, you Hercules, I add.

Darius slow nods, satisfied. *Sooo . . .*
    Drew dips a fry in ketchup. Downs it.
    I dig a thumb into my orange. Tear it.

Darius goes on. *Know what's next, right?*
    Drew stuffs a fry into his mouth. *Nope.*

I split the orange & pop a slice into mine. *Dude, you know
what he's talking about.*
    Just playing. Drew laughs, jaws full of potato. *Yeah I
    know, next record is wheelies.*

Darius swipes one of Drew's fries. *Y'all still down?*
> Drew smacks at his hand. *Dude, shut up, of course we are. Right, I?*

You even gotta ask? Yo, didn't we do the stair-climbing one?—
> I throw a peel.

Didn't we choke down a hundred dry, stale crackers?—
> I throw another.

Hop on one foot?—Another.
> Darius pitches peels back. *Yeah. Yeah. Yeah.*

Well, then. Drew flicks a fry.
> *Fine.* Darius a nugget.

Two seconds later,
we're flinging fries & peels & nuggets until
the girls at the other end sigh & roll their eyes.
> *Chill*, Drew says. Then, on the sly, fires a last fry.

I Bet You

is how it always begins.
No matter the game or record.
One of us'll throw out the first bet,
another'll pick it up & double it,
another'll snatch it back, triple it, like—

Dude, I bet you I'll do thirty seconds over—
Bro, if you doing thirty, I know I'm going like sixty—
Yo, if you got sixty, I know I'll pop at least ninety—

So on & so on
adding time to feats
we ain't hardly gonna reach.
But it's the talking that gets us psyched,
got us believing we got gladiator might.

And it's the believing that counts.

Saturday, March 24

We three ride to Rosewood Lane. Early.
Here, the houses are big.
Yards spring from curbs to far back porches
with birdbaths, lions, & race jockey lawn statues,
with long driveways that lead to two-car garages.
Yo, the kinds of homes Mom stages with plants.

It's quiet. A man walks his Corgi, casually.
Up the street, two ladies push strollers, leisurely.

Cedar Street cuts Rosewood in two,
with cul-de-sacs on each end.
Got no potholes or cracks.
No hills or bumps. No traffic either.
Snow cleared from the street.
Racetrack smooth.

Rock Paper Scissors

We stand in a circle.
Hands jumpy like trigger fingers.

Rock, paper, scissors, shoot—
Drew: *Rock*
Darius: *Paper*
Me: *Paper*
      Mannn, I wanted to set the time, Drew says.
      Why? You ain't going the longest, Darius cracks.

Rock, paper, scissors, shoot—
Darius: *Rock*
Me: *Rock*
      Bro, why we always play the same hand? I say.

Rock, paper, scissors, shoot—
Darius: *Scissors*
Me: *Paper*
      Scissors cut paper. Snip. Snip, Darius rips.

Go!

Yo, we'll go from up there—
Darius points to the cul-de-sac on our end—
to all the way down there—
he points to the other across Cedar—
circle that cul-de-sac and back.

Drew, let me know
when I make three minutes.

Drew throws out his hand.
Yo, you got this. They
front hand slap, back hand slap, dap, dap, palm clasp.

Isaiah, you my eyes, Darius says.
No doubt. We
front hand slap, back hand slap, dap, dap, palm clasp.

And yo, be like water, I tell him.
     Always, he says.

Drew sets the timer.
     Darius rides off.

I jog up the block.
        He pedals & pedals & finally pops
a wheelie.
        My eyes wide for cars.
Drew shouts, *You got this, bro!*
        I yell, *Be like water!*

And dude is going. *Going!* *Going!* **GOING!**

ROAR

Neither me or Drew notice the man bust out his house.
Neither me or Drew see him stomping down his steps.
Neither of us turn from Darius's front wheel twisting &
turning as he balances on his back tire.
No, we don't notice the man until he's in Drew's face.

Hey, what you think you all doing?
the man says. Salty.
  What it look like?
  Drew says. As salty.

Take whatever you're doing and get off my street!
the man yells. Loud.
  You don't own this street!
  Drew yells. As loud.
Curtains spread open.
Front doors too.

  Darius nears the cul-de sac
  Arms out. Balancing! Balancing!

Get outta here before I make you!
the man shouts. Rough.
      We ain't gotta go nowhere!
      Drew shouts. As rough.
Neighbors step on porches.
Some to steps.

      Darius loops the cul-de-sac.
      Tire's up! Steady! Steady!

The man's face is red.
Wrestler veins bulge in his neck.
      Drew's back's to me.
      Boxer fists ball round like stones.

Darius swings our way.
The man scowls & yells.
Drew glowers & roars.
      People surround them.
      Asking. Hissing. Pointing.
      What—who—why?
I gotta go. To Drew. Ball my fists too.
      But—
I gotta watch. Darius coming! Front tire's spinning!
      But—
The man's ranting & frothing.
Drew's steaming & boiling.
People are raving & fuming &
I'm stuck—

I   fight   to   unglue   myself.
Push   through   the   crowd.
Heart   racing   like   a   Derby   horse.

The man surges   then shoves.
Drew stumbles   then I catch
                    then glance back to see

Darius flowing like water.
      A sinking feeling in my gut.
As people crowd.
      As Drew resists.
As the man rages.
      He won't stop raging.
He won't shut up.
      Darius?
           DARIUSSS!
But—
      I scream
CARRR!
      too
late.

Black Hole

Me, Mom, and Dad sit on
the same pew with Drew,
his mom, and his brother.

The preacher preaches of
being in a better place.
A place of no suffering. Or sadness.
He don't know Darius like that.

Darius wasn't suffering. Wasn't sad either.
Wish that preacher would stop his huffing and puffing
of words that don't mean nothing.
Not for Darius.

Drew shifts in his seat, leg bounces
like he's about to kick something.
I fidget with my necktie.
It's squeezing my throat.

A screen drops from the ceiling. Pictures fade one into
another. Darius with his dad . . . mom . . . husky . . .

family members . . . as a baby . . . all the way to eighth
grade . . . and of us cheesing hard, holding our Raspberry Pis.

Mom whispers it's time to say our last goodbye.
We stand in line.
Moans and cries start and stop and start and stop again.
My legs grow heavy. Feet heavier.
The line crawls forward.

The silver casket is in front of me.
My view starts at his hands
crossed one on top of the other and
slowly travels up, as my mind figures out how
to say goodbye to my—best friend.

But I can't. 'Cause I get to his face.
Darius doesn't look like Darius.
Looks like a wax figure of him.

My brain argues that this isn't him.
That this is some weird world record.
But it's not a record. It's not.
I was there. Right there.

Yet still, *still*, I can't say goodbye.

I hug Mr. Goodman. Hug Mrs. Goodman.
She squeezes me tight.

Tears, my tears, build in my eyes.
Tears, my tears, burn, but I won't blink them free.

My tie is too tight.
      Darius is in the casket.
My fingers fight the knot.
      Darius is gone.
This stupid freakin' tie!
      Darius—

Dad moves my hands, loosens the knot,
wraps his arms around my shoulders,
says into my ear,
It'll be okay, Son. It'll be okay.

Crows

We meet outside the church, me and Drew.
All this black. Black everywhere.
Looks like crows. Crying crows.

Drew's eyes are swollen.
Wonder if he's been crying.
Or if they're tears he refuses to let go.
Wonder if he checks his phone as if a text from Darius'll
suddenly appear.
Or if he reads and rereads all the old ones.
Wonder if he replays the scene in his mind over and over
or if it automatically flashes behind his lids when he shuts them,
because . . .
I do.

I lay a hand on his shoulder. *You okay?*
      He shrugs. *Yeah. This all feels—*
Weird, I say, finishing his sentence. *Like it's a—*
      Bad dream. He finishes mine.

Drew closes his eyes, shakes his head like he's back on
Rosewood answering the police officers' questions,

giving them our names and numbers. Back watching
the ambulance put Darius on a stretcher and covering him
with a white sheet. Hearing the repeated apologies of
the driver: *I didn't see him. I'm sorry, I didn't see him.*

After a minute Drew asks, *How you doin'?*
    I shrug.

Drew's brother comes over.
Says it's time to go to the cemetery.
Drew tells him *okay.*
Later, he says to me, then walks away.

Leaves me standing with the crows.

Why?

Dad sits at my desk. Hands folded in his lap.
Doesn't speak. Only sits.
I lie on my bed. Arm covering my eyes.
Don't speak. Until I do.

Me: *That man . . . if it wasn't for him . . . I could've warned . . . it was all my . . .*
Dad: *. . .*
Me: *Yelling at us for being on his street. We weren't even doing nothing wrong.*
Dad: *You didn't do anything wrong. Nothing at all. Neither did Darius. Or Drew.*
Me: *Then why was he so mad? 'Cause now . . . Darius—*
I can't say it. Won't say it.
Dad: *It's . . . complicated. It's . . . ignorance. It's . . .*

Dad struggles to put words together.
I go back to covering my eyes,
knowing nothing he'll say
will ever make me understand *why*.

Post-Darius

Today, my beanie is
pulled down low.
Mom doesn't make me
take it off
inside the house.
Doesn't mention it at all.

Instead, she says,
Isaiah, can you help me clean leaves?
The figs and ZZs lost their shine.

I nod. *Okay.*

My Beanie

Nana gave me my first one when I was in second grade.
My ears were too big for my head.
Kids called me Fat Ears.

Nana said, *Don't worry, you'll grow into them.*
I said, *That'll take forever.*
The next day, she put a knitted hat on my head,
said, *Now they can't see your ears.*

In third fourth fifth sixth grades,
the hat was my cocoon.
If I pulled it down just far enough
I could block out the world.

But I ain't in second grade no more.
Or third, fourth, fifth, sixth, or seventh.
I'm in eighth. So I don't wear it all the time.
Only as an *as needed* thing.

Like I needed it—
when Nana died from heart disease and

there would be no more painting ornaments with her at
Christmas
or when Dad took that new job and is always off
somewhere taking pictures for weeks at a time
or every year on the first day of school, the second and third
days too
or when I fell down that mountain
or when my best friend is gone, and I realize gone is
forever.

School

When the classroom door opens,
I look up. Halfway expecting Darius
to stroll in with a slick smirk on his face.
But no. It's never gon' be him. Ever.

I linger at his locker,
waiting for him to run up spouting
about some anime move he did in PE.
But no. He never comes.

At lunch, me and Drew talk about
what we might do after school. Then
one of us'll look to Darius's empty seat. Then
quickly turn away like we didn't.
Because no. He's not there.

Night Visits

Friday night
a week after the funeral
at 9:33 p.m.
my phone dings.
A text. From Drew. *You up*
Me: *Yeah*
He: *omw*

He started coming sometime last summer.
Sometimes he comes here,
other times he goes—*went*—to Darius's.
I never ask why, what, or nothing.
Just let him in.

Drew noiselessly follows me upstairs,
past my parents' room to mine.
I pull out my sleeping bag and a pillow.
He makes his usual pallet on the floor.

His navy-blue hoodie swallows his head.
He wraps himself cocoon tight.
I stay silent, waiting for him to work out

each knot, looping and unlooping, until
whatever's got him tied up unravels.

Once, it was because his brother got scary sick.
Another time, his dad's assignment to Serbia—or was it Syria?
Something like that—got extended.

The last time, his brother was finally diagnosed.
Sickle cell. Means Marvin's red blood cells
get all blocked, can't get to his veins, stops the oxygen
from getting to his organs. Yeah, scary sick.

But this time, I bet—
it's about Darius.

Again

Mom doesn't ask me
to take off my hat.
Instead, she says,
Isaiah,
can you help me
water the plants?
The African mask's leaves
look a little limp.

I nod. *Fine.*

It's Been Two Weeks
and still between classes, in the halls,
kids drop their eyes and pretend
they don't see us—
"the friends of the boy
who was killed."

Others who probably didn't know Darius,
who hardly talk to me or Drew,
still pester us with questions.

In PE, this boy Quinton asks,
>*Why was he riding over there anyway?*

In geography, this kid Maleek asks,
>*What kind of car was it?*

At lunch, this girl Trina asks,
>*What was the man saying?*

Our throats grow tired of answering questions.
Until
finally
in the middle of the hallway
between fourth and fifth periods

after being asked what happened for the hundredth time
Drew flips out—

I'm done talking about it! Leave me alone!
He falls quiet. His eyes go dark.

But what I didn't know was
his "done talking about it"
included me too.

Been Fifteen Days Since

the funeral and
Mom doesn't tell me it's time
I take off my hat inside the house
or her greenhouse
where
I propagate a snake plant by
carefully trimming the leaves
to cut V shapes at the bottoms
to place in jars of water
where
I repeat with more leaves that
in a few weeks will
shoot new roots from their stems
where
I now gather handfuls of soil in my palms
crush the dirt tight between my fingers
and hold it.
        Hold it. Breathe.
Naw,
Mom doesn't tell me it's time
I finally take off my hat—
she doesn't have to.
        It's here, though. As needed.

Four Weeks Post-Funeral

Me & Drew hang out in front of my house.
His neck slumped down. Locs freshly shaven.
Thumb swiping faster & faster on his phone's screen.
He doesn't notice the sun creeping across the sky,
hauling away another weekend of doing nothing.

My feet balance on my board, rocking side to side,
waiting for Drew to kick up his board too, & bet
I can't do some wild trick. But his head stays down.

Five minutes ago, dude wouldn't shut up about
pulling a levitation prank on his mom.
Talking about how I should prank my mom too.
Then I said, *I could see Darius doing that, can't you?*
Now, now his lips are magnet tight.

Now he's a new Drew.
A no-talking Drew.
A silently scroll-through-his-phone Drew.
I throw up my hands like, *Really, dude?*

Sup? I ask.
Nothin', he answers.

I wait for him to start yapping again.
He doesn't.

I stuff my hands into my pockets,
go back to rocking while Drew's steadily swiping.

Yeah, I hate when things change. Like, the time I
was finally okay with my tablemates & Mr. Hart
rearranged seats to "change things up."

Or when Mom switched spaghetti & meatballs
to a healthier spaghetti & black-bean-chickpea balls.

Or how Drew can go from clowning
to silence in seconds.

It's because of me. Bringing up Darius.
So now I tuck my thoughts inside
like a turtle in its shell.
I hop on the hood of Mom's car, lie back &
picture myself floating after the sun
       high
          High
             HIGHER.

Flying past stars,
chilling on Mars, &
zipping back
in time to—
Hey, here's one, I say, suddenly thinking of a game

we play with Darius—my throat gets funeral-tie-knot tight
because it's one we *used to play* with Darius.

So yeah, it's a game where we ask each other stupid
random questions, demanding quick honest answers.
The rules: you can't stall, say *um*, or answer with a question.
Otherwise, the asker gets to tag you.

I slide off the car. *If you could choose a superpower right now,
at this very moment, what would it be?*

Drew holds his phone mid-air. *Easy. I'd manipulate time.*
Boom. He's in.
Drew asks what movie I'd star in.

I pause three seconds too long. He tags my arm.
I fight against rubbing it & lose. *Oww. Dang, bro.*
I massage the spot. *Was about to say* Jade Dynasty.
What's the worst thing you can break?

Easy. Marvin's console.
I laugh. *Yeah, he'd put the paws on you.*
He asks, *What girl in school would you step to?*
I think. Drew tags.

Dude! I rub my arm again. *Name a favorite celeb.*
Drew hesitates. I raise my fist, ready, when he warns,
Bet not laugh.

Why would I?
Drew says, *Taimak.*
Taimak? I repeat. *Last Dragon Taimak?*

> *The Last Dragon* is an old kung fu flick
> we've watched at least twenty times.

What else he's been in? I snort. *Dude—*
What? Drew side-eyes me. *Something funny?*
I didn't laugh. *Why would that be funny?*

Drew tells me how someone told him only girls, &
guys who dig guys, like Taimak. Dude's a pretty boy.

That's dumb, I scoff. *A pretty boy who can probably
lay that "someone" out flat. 'Sides, ain't like it's Patti LaBelle.*

Drew echoes, *Patti who?*

Pause for Patti

With him being all touchy about Taimak
no way I'm telling how
when I was seven
I first heard
a Patti LaBelle song.
That was the day
Dad told Mom
I needed to be toughened up.
See, I spent a whole week putting together
an 850-piece puzzle of the galaxy.
Mom came home from work
exactly when I snapped
the last shape into place &
she put on a playlist
to celebrate.
I jumped up dancing victory over that puzzle—
yo, it was *hard*.
We danced together until Mom laughed,
Isaiah, I can't keep up with you,
not in these heels.
I said, *They don't look too hard to dance in to me.*

Mom shed her shoes. *Here,*
you try if that's what you think.
I slipped them on, got my balance, &
she & me danced together,
until
Dad spouted,
Kay!
Isaiah is not your daughter.
He
is our son.
He gotta be toughened up.
My lips quivered, my eyes welled up, &
Dad said to me,
Big boys don't cry.
I was only seven.
How was I supposed to know that
dancing with Mom
in her shoes
to a Patti LaBelle song
& crying about it
wasn't tough?

Questions, Cont'd

I wave Drew off. *Ay, what's up with the haircut?*
       He rubs his scalp & explains how his mom wants
       him to look more "presentable." *Like I wasn't already.*
I shake my locs outta my face. *That's wild.*

Drew looks to the sky as if he finally noticed
it's gotten dark. *Yo, I gotta bounce.*

We go inside to tell Mom bye.
       She grabs her purse & keys. *I'll take—*
Drew interrupts, *That's okay, Mrs. Randolph. I'm good.*
       Boy, snaps Mom. *You're not walking home alone.*
       It's dark.
Mrs. Randolph, he says, deadpan. *Whatever can happen to
me at night can happen in the day.*
       Her mouth turns in, chews on his words. *True,* she
       comes back with, *but it won't happen on my watch.*
       Now get in the car.

We three pile into Mom's car.
Not even two minutes pass before
she glances into the rearview mirror &

tells Drew how much she likes his haircut.
Her eyes cut to my aloe-vera-looking locs.

She stops at a stop sign & starts again. *I bet your mom loves it too. Oh, is she liking the plant I sent over?*
      Yes, ma'am, he says.
Ma'am? I almost spin in my seat. When did Drew get all *yes, ma'am–y*?

We turn into his apartment complex.
Mom slowly weaves through the lot.
Would you like a plant for yourself?

Me? Drew's voice goes up as if to say, *What I look like with a plant?* Instead, he says, *I'll pass.*

Four boys stand in the way like they got bumpers.
At the last minute, they jump to the side.
Mom shakes her head. *The way cars speed through here, I pray none of these kids get hurt.*

Get hurt.   *Darius.*
I turn away, face the window.

Mom puts the car in park. Drew jumps out with
a rushed *Thank you* as I try to dislodge the *bye*
from behind my tonsils but it's jammed just like
my mind is on *that* day.

The Photographer's Eye

It's been almost five weeks since Dad was last home.
The funeral. Now he's here for five days. Saturday,
we go downtown to take pics of what catches our eye.
Joe Louis's fist, Comerica Park's tiger statues,
old men collecting pop bottles in trash bags,
blinking lights in Trappers Alley,
sun breaking through clouds,
pigeons pecking on curbs,
the Renaissance Center.

Let me see. Good, adjust the focus.
Wow, look how the light frames the top of the building.

In between camera clicks, I debate telling Dad how
I'm still struggling with . . . you know . . .

He takes a pic of a bird resting on Joe Louis's knuckle.
Then pauses. *You're not snapping. You good?*

Yeah. I lift the camera to my eye. Lower it. *No.*
I tell him my feels, then hope he doesn't say
what adults usually say. *He's in a better place.*

Dad lets his camera hang from the strap.
He lays both hands on my shoulders.
Grief, he says, *is one of those emotions that'll consume you,
if you don't take care of yourself. Trust me, I know.*

He gazes off as if daydreaming. Just when I figure it's back
to snapping, Dad says, *Isaiah, it's okay to feel bad. There's no
time limit to it.*

No time limit? I can't go on like this for forever.
Wanting to talk about Darius. Talk about *that* day.
Wanting to ask Drew if he blames me for yelling *car*
too late. Ask if he's mad at all.

Can't. Not when he always goes silent like
he wants to forget it. And I can't just forget it.
So tell me, how am I supposed to get over feeling bad
when I can't even talk about it?

The Last Dragon

    Drew's
at the door talking about *Let's watch* The Last Dragon.
Got us mad dashing to the basement, where
the flat-screen is mounted high on the wall.
This was Dad's man cave until Mom said, *What's a cave
without plants?* Now it's Mom's mom cave.

    Drew
casts himself as quest-seeking Leroy Green, aka
Bruce Leeroy, like always. Darius *was*—
& now Drew wants *me* to be—
the evil warrior Sho'nuff, aka the Shogun of Harlem.
Which feels weird. I tell Drew we should probably
stream something else. *Bruh,* he says, *can we just
watch this?* We stand stiff for a minute, then finally I say,
Okay,

    because
when I push play, we'll time travel back to when
me, he, & Darius sparred in my backyard,
where we practiced tae kwon do moves
side kicked punks through windows

knocked knuckleheads with nunchucks &
served up nighty-night-sleep-tight juice
like we hood heroes.

    We
now act the lines at the same time
as they filter through the speakers
because in our space we're down to do
what most kids from school wouldn't dare do
for fear of being called out for pretending to be anything
other than who we pretend to be. Good thing, 'cause
Drew's finally hiccup-laughing & I'm hiccup-laughing too.

    By
the end of the movie, Drew wipes sweat from his brow—
air all sliced with roundhouse kicks &
me, Shogun, laid out, butt whooped—&
admits, *This'll never get stale*. I wanna bring up Darius
so bad, but bite it back because this Drew,
right here, is the old Drew. &
I hope this door'll stay open
till the time limit of us feeling
bad
is closed.

Field Trip

      Days later,
on our eighth-grade field trip to Marshall High, we walk
through halls full of giant football-playing-looking dudes
with mustaches & beards—*beards, yo!* Girls I'll never
ever have the nerve to step to & teachers whose faces are
chiseled with *I don't play*. This school is monstrously huge.
Like, three stories high & two blocks long huge. Like, get
lost every day in a different hallway huge.

      Come September,
we'll be guppies surrounded by sharks. What if they sniff out
the real me? I've seen what happens to dudes like me in high
school. Seen it play out in the movies. Comic-book geeking
secretly plant-liking can't-shoot-a-free-throw dudes get stuffed
in lockers. Gym clothes stolen. Left to run around naked. That's
what happens. Like I said, seen it play out.

      I whisper
to Drew. *Dude, so not ready for this. You?*
Drew's eyes lie when he shrugs me off with a *Yeah, man.*

On the bus ride back,
everybody's wild, leaning over seats talking mad loud.
Drew stares out the window, brushing his hair. His new
hobby for his new look. What if this new Drew gets
even newer come fall? Too new for old me? I push it
from my mind & rewind my Shogun impression,
which had us rolling. I squint one eye, bulge the other,
& turn to Drew. *Now, when I say who's the master,
you say Sho'nuff—*

    Drew grins
for a millisecond. Then it fades. *Come on, bro, you know
we can't keep acting like li'l kids.*

    Just
this weekend it was all good. But now, all of a sudden, Drew's
wipe-his-hands done with this "kid"stuff. Got me scratching
my head like *Wha?*

Vintaged

My 1993 Aerosmith concert tee finally came. Today!
Yo, it's got a skull & crossbones over wings.
Gold-green snakes on each side flicking pink tongues.
Gnarly bone hands wielding daggers.
Red ghostly writing over gold banners.
Little wear. Little fading. Supreme!

I pull it over my head, gentle. "Walk This Way" blasts.
Dope pose in the mirror. Rock sign to the ceiling.
Head bangs. Until the song ends.
Then quick, take it off. Costs too much to get it sweaty.

I go to stash my tee—trip over my sneaks spread over the
closet floor; step over the box of comics I've been
meaning to move—way in the back of my closet.

Yeah okay, looks like I'm hiding it. I'm not.
Just private. That's all.

It's Not Forever Yet

In my basement, Drew blocks the TV screen,
mimicking Ip Man's leg sweep

while I pretend not to hear the *tick-tick-tick* countdown to
our last day of school eighteen days away. But dag,
the *tick* is loud.

Ip Man's got one fist out, the other close to his chest,
ready to take down the ten guys circling him.
It dawns on me that *The Last Dragon* is the *only*
martial arts movie we've watched with Black fighters.

You know—I balance on my right foot, raise my left knee,
draw my arms above my head—*Taimak's probably the first
Black man to do kung fu in a movie.*

No, he's not. Drew jab-jab-kicks.
Might've been Kareem Abdul-Jabbar. Ha!
Trained by Bruce Lee himself. Ha!
Starred in Game of Death. *Huh!*
Legs this long. Hie!
No, longer than . . . the couch . . .

I drop my stance, totally shocked.
How you know all that?

He holds his pose; fists block his eyes. *Dude,
I ain't tell you my father's a black belt in karate?*

Drew once told me his dad nerds out over *The Last Dragon*.
Same with *Shaolin Style* on the PlayStation too.
But a black belt?

Naw.—I kick, punch.—*Never told me that.*
Yep. Drew swipes the air, drops to a sumo stance.

Kareem's probably the tallest, though. Dude's probably tall as—
he pauses to think—*the top of your kitchen cabinets. Hi-ya!*

Wait, I say, already forgetting about Drew's dad.
Taller than our cabinets? Nuh-uh.
He says, *Uh-huh. How much you wanna bet?*
We shake.
If I lose, I decide, *you can hold my Switch for a week. If I win—*
Drew snorts. *Dude, you won't win.*

We race upstairs to the kitchen's junk drawer.
We find—
          Scotch tape & a spool of thread
            magnets & sticky notes
        business cards & paper clips &
     way in the back . . . the measuring tape.

Drew holds one end.
I climb onto the counter & reach.

How tall is it? he asks.
Six feet ten inches. I hop down before Mom can bust me
standing in my dirty, germy sneakers on her
Clorox-clean counters.

On my phone we search Kareem's stats &
discover he was
seven foot two inches &
the first Black martial arts film star was not
Kareem Abdul-Jabbar but
six-foot-two Jim Kelly.
In *Enter the Dragon*.

We forget about measuring—
forget about the bet—
forget about practicing our moves—
because we have to watch the man who
drop-kicked villains before
Taimak &
Kareem Abdul-Jabbar
ever did.

Night Visit

9:28 p.m.
Drew texts: *omw*.
I open the door. Again.
He's in the sleeping bag on my floor. Again.
Silence.
            Silence.
                        Silence.

About six thousand hours go by, then
Drew's voice breaks through the darkness.
My ears become antennae.

Sometimes I wish . . .
I wait, soundlessly, for Drew to unscramble his thought.
. . . my pops was here.

He's missing his dad. I get it.
His dad's been away for, dang, how many months now?
Heck, my dad's only been gone for three days &
I feel the same.

Drew goes back quiet again.
Not sure what to say, so I ask,
When's he coming home?

He oun't know yet. Drew rolls over.
The sleeping bag swishes.

I picture his father protecting government officials,
on overseas missions, saluting in his army uniform.
Breaking out a black belt move every now & then.

It goes noiseless again. Except for the distant dog bark.
I wait &
        wait &
                wait
                      for Drew to finish.

About another six thousand hours go by & then I hear
his deep breathing.

Knockout

As I put away my lunch tray,
Mr. Hart stops me to ask how I am.
I know he's asking how's life without Darius.
How am I supposed to answer that?
So I simply say, *Fine*.

Outside, I look for Drew.
He's at the court with Marcus & Randy
sharing a bag of Takis, watching kids
wait in line hoping to sink a free throw
faster than their opponent. Yeah, knockout.

Hey, I say.
Yo. Aye from Randy & Drew.
Whassup, Flower Boy from Marcus.
Yo, I pick one oxalis during a football game way back
in fifth grade & ever since I'm freakin' Flower Boy?
Like I'm soft or something. 'Sides, oxalis are weeds. Weeds!

A kid scores. All three yell, *Yeah!*
I watch the game too, but then
peep how Drew's brush waves

now match Randy's & Marcus's.
All three wear Jordans too.
All three dig red-stained fingertips into the bag.
Whoa, is Drew finding a new duo to make a trio?

It hits me.
Yo, are *they* why
he's all
Can't be acting like li'l kids now?

They Real Cool

See, *for real* for real,
with his now close fade & clean Jays
this new Drew can easily slip to the
other side. The
cool side. The
hype side. The
ball-dunking & touchdowning side. The
anything-but-skateboarding Vans-wearing "flower"-plucking
me side.
With Darius gone & now him with them . . .
I can't help but wonder
if Drew's about to slide.

Rosewood Lane

After school, I stroll home in the misty rain.
Hardly pay it attention because my mind's cruising
back to how I used to always walk home with Darius.

As Bad Brains scream in my ears,
I suddenly realize I'm at the corner of
Rosewood Lane.

Up the block is where *it* happened. Darius planned
the route, the time, the smoothest ground. Everything.
That's how he was. If he liked something, he studied it.

Like, really studied it. Take comics. Dude was
da gawd of nerddom. Biggest comics head ever. EVAH.
Knew Marvel's & DC's universes like he had dual citizenship.

If I squint, I can make out where he took off.
If I could, I'd go there. Rewind the time to
before the ambulance drove him away
before the police asked hundreds of questions
before the car turned
before the crowd crowded

before the man yelled &
bring Darius right back to us rock paper scissors–ing.

If I could just go down there. Maybe—
but my feet won't budge.
Yeah, I choke. Okay, okay, I know—
But my feet still won't go.

Flipping Bottles

Today, after lunch, we lean on the wall watching
the new crew at the Four Square Corner.

Drew sips water, caps it,
throws his bottle in the air, catches it.
Throws, catches.

His throwing reminds me of
Darius & the time this kid Julius bet he couldn't
flip his bottle five times in a row.

Without flinching, Darius was like, *Bet*.
He didn't make five times. Only two.
But from that moment, dude practiced & practiced
until he could land a straight ten.

That one word got him bottle flipping,
got us record breaking,
got my memories churning,
got me thinking . . .

Bet. Bottle Flip. Records.

I say to Drew, *You catch that bottle like you got skills.*
He scoffs. *Got more than that.*
Figured he'd say that, so I throw a line.
Bet you can't flip it on its bottom ten times in a row.
Bruh—he pushes off the wall—*how much you wanna bet?*
Boom. Bait snagged.

                        Bet. Bottle flip. Records. . . .

Next thing, Drew is crouched low, laser focused,
holding the bottle by its neck.
He flips. Misses. *Dang!*
Flips again. Misses. *Dag!*
Flips. Makes it. *Yes!*
Time for fifth period. Kids march toward the doors.
Drew keeps flipping.
I say, *You know who made ten?*
Who? he says, without looking up.
Darius.
Drew stops flipping.

                        Bet. Bottle flip. Records. . . .

Mr. Brown tells us to hurry to class.
Drew tosses the plastic into the recycling bin,
pulls out his brush, & walks off.
Hold up, I call out.
He doesn't hold up. So I catch up.

                        Bet. Bottle flip. Records. . . .

At our locker, we textbook grab & notebook snatch.
I was thinking, I hesitate. *This summer, we should start back up . . . the records.*
Kids scurry by. Mr. Brown warns us to not be late.
Drew brushes straight strokes. *Why?*

Whys: so we can talk about Darius without lip seals; so we stay boys. Bet neither of these are the whys Drew wants to hear. Instead, I say, *So we can, you know, have an epic summer. Before the fall.*

Epic summer? He closes the locker. *Nah, I'm good.*
Naw? Because of . . . of—
Nah, he says over his shoulder. *'Cause it's not my thing no more.*
I throw up my hands. *Bro, seriously? What's your thing? 'Cause I don't know.*
Drew stops for a second to say, *I oun't either.*

Motivation

A few days later, almost everybody's crammed
in the media center to escape the rain.
I'm here for record-breaking books.

Mrs. Rice informs me most have been lost or never returned.
She loans me two & promises to order more.

I take one. Drew takes the other.
We sit at a table off to the side in view of the door.
That's when Vanessa enters with her friends.
His eyes go wide.

According to Drew, Vanessa is the finest girl at Oakdale.
He likes when she wears Air Force 1s with denim skirts.
Likes her long braids threaded with different colors.
Been crushing on her for a year. Always been two inches
too short to step to her. Until now.

Dude, I say. *And you say I choke.*
Shut up. He flips a page like he's reading.
Bet you won't ask for her number, I dare.
Drew glares at me. Huffs. Huffs again. *Aight. Bet.*

Vanessa passes our table
stops   backs up
reads the title of the book in Drew's hand
& says,   *Cool.*

Drew mumbles something incoherent to
Vanessa's back.
Immediately turns to me & says,
Dude, I want in.

Nuh-uh, I say.
Nuh-uh? he echoes.
Shock-faced, Drew slumps in his chair
& sneaks peeks at Vanessa.

Dude, for Vanessa? Or—I pause—*brohood?*
Drew glances at Vanessa, back at me,
once more at Vanessa, finally back to me, & says,
Both?

On a Mission

Not because of me
or us being boys
or my supe idea for an "epic summer"
but
because of Vanessa,
we find ourselves skating down my block
Mom's safety warnings on our backs
flying through the neighborhood
across Montgomery Street & straight to the
public library on a Saturday when we should be doing
anything else like playing ball or playing a different ball game
or the kinds of video games Drew's brother
commands control over.
We leap the library stairs by twos,
shoving our way inside at the same time
laughing at Drew's stuck arm & my bumped head
as the lady behind the counter glares.

Nah, this only happens when you & your homie
are on a mission. A Guinness World Record mission.

The Scrolls

As if they were ancient scrolls holding great secrets,
the librarian tells us that years ago
Guinness World Record books had waiting lists.

First thing we do is verify the rules, i.e.,
parental permission is required, which I agree to ask Mom.

It's not fair. Darius should be here.
But I won't go soft, nah; I make myself Hulk hard
as we flip through page after page
year after year
gathering ideas.

I show Drew a picture of a guy with tattoos
over his entire body. Dragons eagles women webs
flaming skulls American flags too.

Drew jokes, *Dude probably got 'em on his butt. Bet he didn't
sit for a week. Speaking of butts, check out this lady's fingernails.*
He adds, *Bruh, how she wipe?*

Her nails are so long they curl into crescent moons twice over.
I answer, *Very carefully.*
Old Drew bursts out laughing.

We find records for the
> Longest-lashes person
> Most-hot-dog-eating person
> Most-pins-in-face person
> Largest Afro & smallest-eyes persons
> Smallest human & biggest-nose persons
> Biggest hands & fattest cat
> Fattest alligator & highest climb
> & highest high-top fade too.

We aren't the tallest or the shortest.
> The thinnest or the thickest.
We can't high jump or somersault
> over & over.
We aren't & can't do none of this stuff.

> *Daaaaaaaang,* I grumble. *What we gon' do?*

Mom and Dad

Dad calls home.
He asks how I'm feeling about Darius.
I don't know what to say. I tell him, *Better.*
He promises to be home in two weeks
for my graduation.
I say, *It's no big deal.*
He insists it *is* a big deal.

      That night, after dinner, from my spot at the sink,
                        hands swishing in suds,
               I overhear Mom on the phone
        with my uncle and aunt from North Carolina.
She says Dad hasn't been the same since investigators let
      that boy from Missouri lie in the street for hours.

Told them Dad couldn't cry, even though he wanted to
          when he entered Emmanuel Baptist Church,
     where the gunman killed all those worshippers
             for the same reason they bombed
                  the Birmingham church in 1963.

Told them my father's old boss assigned him to all the
Black issue stories because he could
authentically cover the Black experience.
But every story was about
blood, bullets, and beatless hearts.

I flash back to those days.
Those days, he'd sometimes come home,
call me to the table excited to show
pictures he took on his own of
Black lives like—
Boys grandstanding on dirt bikes
Girls Double Dutching in front of brownstones
Fraternities and sororities stomping the yard as the
marching bands go hard at HBCUs
Line dancing dancers and two-stepping couples
gliding satin smooth
House music deejays dropping beats for partiers
to dance all night
Roller skaters soaring like freedom on eight wheels
Go-go bands bringing the funk
Cowboys and cowgirls wrangling at the rodeo—

But Dad said
none of these were
the authentic Black experiences
his boss wanted to see.

Mom tells Aunt Terri and Uncle Vent she's glad
his new job at *National Geographic* has given him
a much-needed change,
that yes, he's doing better, and his contract
will be ending soon, if he doesn't renew.

Hold up, *if he* doesn't *renew?*

Pause

Mom and I fall back, letting our bodies be swallowed up
by recliners for our Sunday-afternoon movie ritual.
Last time it was my choice—*Spider-Man*. Yeah, again.
Today's hers.

She sifts through at least a hundred movies in her saved list
while ragging about my hair getting out of control.
Pfft. It's her to-watch list that's outta control.

People'll think you're a thug, she says.
It's not that bad, I assure her. *'Sides, think I'm going for a
Basquiat look.*
She squints at me. *Which one?*

I sneeze. Mom reminds me to take my allergy meds.
I'm not a baby, I remind her.
You're my baby, she reminds *me*.

I'm burning to ask if Dad's renewing his job,
but she'll give me the *you've been listening to my
conversations* look. Then it'll get serious when I just
wanna chill.

Mom chooses *The Photograph*. Five minutes in,
I can tell it's not gonna be funny. She paints her nails and says
how cute the guy lead is. Says his hair's nice too.

Mom, I groan. Now she's got me thinking about my hair and
Drew's cut. Which reminds me to ask her for parental
permission for our mission. Guinness rules.

Sure, but what will you two be doing exactly?
She holds up her hand, admiring.

Haven't figured that out. But we're working on it.
Nice, I compliment her nails.

The color is the deepest purple I've ever seen.
Purple so deep it could've been siphoned from the galaxy.
Purple so purple Prince would've written a song about it.
Purple so black it looks like magic.

The polish is slick on her nails like honey.
I joke she can shoot sparkles from her fingertips,
already imagining the flames I'd shoot from mine.

Just as quick, seven-year-old me comes crashing in
in Mom's heels, stomping all over with
He gotta be toughened up, Kay.

Mom. I hesitate. *You think it'd be weird . . .*
if I tried polish?

She pauses. A pause so small
I don't think she even realizes it. *No, not at all.*

But was her pause the real answer?

Lessons

Mom once told me she always wanted a girl,
to teach her to be
brave
bold &
fierce.
That's what she told me.

But God saw fit to
take away one of my X
chromosomes. Turn it Y.

Guess those lessons . . .
                those lessons
weren't meant for
                me.

Curious

Later, I get Mom's polish. Unscrew the top.
Pull out the brush. Dab my toes.
My fingers shake. But I keep dabbing.

I go to my closet &
stand before the Rock Gawds
with my Midnight Purple–painted toes.
      I am
         a cooler me.
A *Tougher Than Leather* Run-D.M.C. me.
A rock along to AC/DC *Back in Black* me.
A punk rocker emocore me.
A *this is who I really am & I like it* me.
Then I hear Marcus & Randy—
        wannabe-white-boy-Black—

& I'm 100 percent sure I don't want anyone to ever see
this purple-polish side
      of me.

So, This Happened:
Drew told the librarian Mrs. Rice that me & him will break
world records—yes, with an *s*—over the summer.

Now she's announcing it on the loudspeaker.
For the morning news. *The morning news!*
Give a big Bronco cheer to Drew Murphy and
Isaiah Randolph—

Immediately, hands stop signing yearbooks
as heads swivel my way. My dome drops
to the desk with a thud. *Nooo.*
Even Mr. Hart gives a slow clap & nod.

After class, kids surround me like reporters.
What y'all gon' do?   My hands go clammy.
You even good at anything? My mouth goes dry.
Why world records?   Darius is why.

Everybody's crammed in the hallways,
joking, laughing, & dapping, while Drew floats
to our locker riding a cloud of claps

with a hand outstretched, signing yearbooks
like a celebrity. *Bruh,* he says when he reaches me.
Guess who got Vanessa's number?

Drew's never spoken more than five words to her.
You got her number? How?

He brushes while boasting about her hearing the
announcement. *She was like, Wow, that's so impressive.
Yo, look what she signed in my book—*
> *To Drew, A boy with a cute smile. K.I.T.*
> *xoxo, Vanessa*

Kids clean out lockers. Paper litters the floor.
I grip my yearbook & gripe, *Dude, why'd you tell?
We don't even know what we gon' do.*

Drew says, *Listen, I'll make a list.
You make a list. We'll put our lists together. Boom.
Done, fam.* He smiles at Vanessa. *Here, sign my book.*

Yeah, right. Done. I take his book, hand him mine,
flip the pages, past the faces with braces & cheesing
mouths, & past the club & sport teams too.

I don't mean to, but do,
finger straight down our class pics
& stop at *Goodman,* to where

Darius is locked in a small square photo.
It's not fair.
It's *not* fair.

I write my name on the last page.
Swap back books with Drew as he signs & flirts.
Then I slip by the selfie takers, singers, huggers, & criers, & disappear down the hall.
Alone.

Surprise

I get home from school, turn my key in the lock, and—*swoosh!* The door swings open so fast the handle yanks outta my hand. *What the—*
I go Bruce Lee. *Hiieyaa!*
    Whoa, Son. Don't hurt the air.

Dad? Really? I breathe out, pretending he didn't almost stop my heart. Pretending I'm not pumped to see him.

He pulls me in for a bear hug. *Missed you.*
Yeah, me too. I hug him back.

Mom comes down the steps, eyes beaming.
He'll be fourteen soon and already catching up to you.

Dad pushes me to arm's length. He's six three and always seemed like a giant. Where I'm all twisty-tie thin, he's hard-to-knock-down solid. The top of my head brushes near his shoulder. *Yeah, you are.*
    My chest swells all on its own.

I hurry upstairs, and in five minutes, I've kicked off my sneaks, changed into my inside clothes, and slipped my dogs into my slides. Can't have Mom fussing about me lying around in my outside stuff.

Dad's at the dining room table, computer open, describing the exotic places he's traveled to, the once-in-a-lifetime photos he's taken. He gets to the last one, runs out of things to say, and notices his son has purple-painted toes.

Dag.
Dad looks at my toes,
      looks at me,
down at my toes,
      up at me.

I become X-Men's Professor X
to read his mind. But he's
helmet-wearing Magneto, blocking me out.

At least, that's what I pretend,
even though there's no point
in pretending at telepathy.
Dad's superpower is speaking his mind.

And mine seems to be
being seven years old, 'cause
I'm right back there again. Waiting for—
He's gotta be toughened up. . . .

Cool, Not Cool

Dad says something that shocks me.
He says, *Cool.*
That's exactly what he says. *Cool.*

He zips to his computer, searching, explaining how he's taken photos of ancient male Egyptians with stained nails. *Different colors meant different statuses, like, black meant higher class. . . .*
    I flex my toes.

They're cool on your feet, Son, but you don't wear it on your fingers, do you?
    I curl my toes.

Dad starts again. *Isaiah, I'm not saying for you not to be you. I'm just saying . . .*
His mouth twists. Eyebrows furrow.

This is exactly why I didn't want no one to see *me* me.

'Saiah. He interrupts my thoughts. *It's just that you're a Black boy. And . . . I don't want anyone to have another reason to question you.*

But, Dad, I say. *It's just . . . paint.*

Girls

can use power tools,
wear blue, play football and hockey,
box, wrestle, drive race cars too. Girls can
be firefighters, construction workers, police, and
security guards. Girls can pretend, dress up, play with
dolls, without ever being too old. They can be brave
or scared, cry without being told to stop. They can
even do karate! Girls can feel or not.
They can *not* wear polish, dresses,
or heels, and still be
girls.

But . . .
it's a big deal if boys wear polish.

Bye, Basquiat Hair

At breakfast, I'm still digesting what Dad said.
The worry in his voice gets me thinking.
Thinking that maybe it's kinda like the worry I have
if my boys saw polish on me. *Kinda.*

Mom untwists the loaf of bread's twisty thingy.
Want a slice?
It's got so many seeds we can plant a piece in the yard
and up'll pop a sunflower garden. *No thanks.*

Dad waltzes in, says to me, *You ready?*
Mom answers, *Yes! He should get it low like yours.*

Dad has a baldie. Nothing wrong with a baldie. But
with his beard, it's like all his hair ran from the top of
his head to the bottom of his face. *No way!* I say.

They laugh like it's funny. It's not *that* funny.

Barbershop Blues

Dad and I sit in a crowded barbershop.
He asks what cut I'm getting.
Wanna say none. I look around for clues.
Guys get low fades, short fros,
kinky fros, high-top fades too.
Some, razor-sharp edges framing foreheads.
Others, straight lines, wavy lines, braids, and baldies.

A seat opens. I hop in.
The barber covers me with a cape.
His foot pumps a bar. I rise.
He asks what I want.
My finger points to a poster on the wall that
displays different styles, from dreadlocks to
neat church-boy cuts. All numbered.
I choose wild loc styles.
Either number four or number nine.

Dad clears his throat and pipes,
His mother would be happier with a three or an eleven.

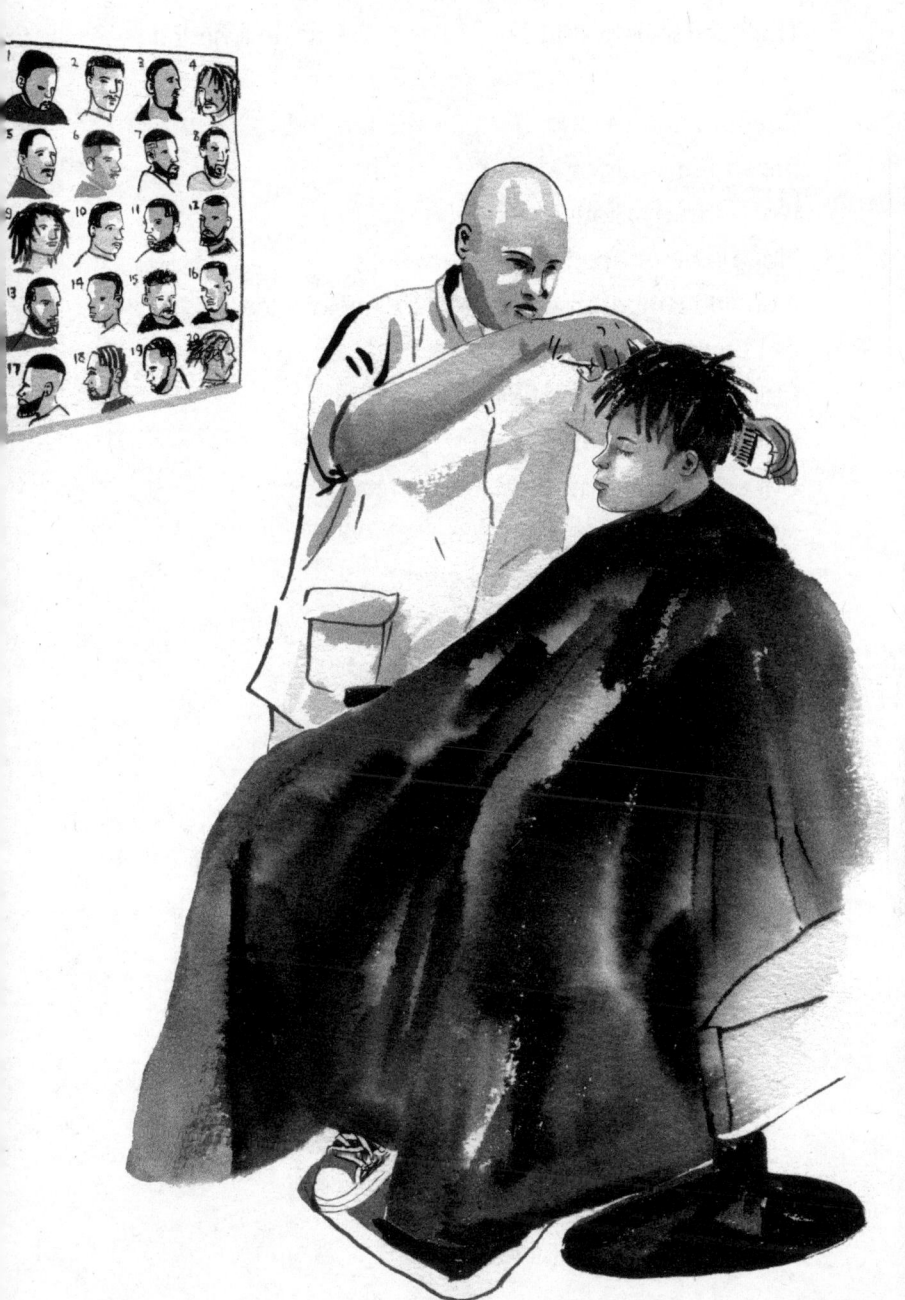

Three or eleven? Naw, I spit.
We haggle like two lawyers.
The barber sighs and says, *I got it. Let me do what I do.*

Twenty minutes later, he spins me around,
hands me a mirror.
Not a three or four.
Not a nine or an eleven.
Not wild rubber-tree locs beating my forehead
as I bang to a drum solo.
Or overgrown twisty foliage, caged in
by neatly tapered sides.
But an in-between—top locs trimmed,
sides and back cut low.
A just right.

Graduation Day

Can't tie my tie. Should know how.
Just wore one ten weeks ago. Darius's funeral.

Dad stands behind me. His hands guide mine as we
face the mirror. He tells me how proud he is of me.

We line up to march into the auditorium.
Drew clocks my new cut, smirks. *Yo!*
I grin. *Yeah.*

Everybody checks out everybody as if we're not all
covered in black gowns and caps with gold tassels.

There're a few songs. Few speeches. Few droopy eyes
and rubbery necks. The graduation music begins.

Cheers and whistles from families as each of us, one
after the other, stroll across the stage, shake a hand, and
is awarded a scroll.

What gets me hyped is Dad's clicking finger capturing shots
with every turn. And Mom's big smile and waving hand.

I glance at Drew. He keeps peeking back as if any second
his father'll bust through the double doors.
His brother drapes an arm around their mother's shoulders.
She dabs a balled-up tissue to her eyes.

Can't believe I told Dad graduation was no big deal.
I catch his eye, give him a chin up.
He returns one back, except he doesn't even know why.

Principal Freeman stands at the podium. Announces
it's awards and presentation time. Beginning with an
honorary diploma for
                        Darius Goodman.

Darius? I crane my neck, peering around,
when I spot his parents.

Mr. Goodman leads Mrs. Goodman carefully up the steps
and across the stage. Principal Freeman gives them a diploma.
Darius's mother chokes back a sob.

Principal Freeman asks for thirty seconds of silence.
I offer more.

Rosewood

I go to Rosewood. Again. On purpose.
Sometimes it doesn't feel real. Him gone.
Sometimes it seems like there's something more,
something I need to do for him. To let him know
I'll be okay, he'll be okay, we all will be okay.
But for real, I don't even know if that's true.

At graduation, Mrs. Goodman let out a sob
that echoed through the entire auditorium.
Like she'd been holding it in for years.
Darius's father rubbed her back with
tears dripping from his chin.
For the rest of the ceremony, I could still hear that sob.

He should've been here to walk across the stage.
To sign yearbooks. To pop that wheelie.
Darius was on a mission.
To be the greatest. *The greatest.*
And I guess I keep coming back to remind him
he is.

Late Texts

Tonight, my phone buzzes.
Drew: *omw*

This time,
        there's no twisting or turning.
This time,
        Drew is zombie still.
This time,
        it could be about his father . . . or Darius.
This time,
        I wake up to find Drew already gone.

Freedom

The first day of summer is an official do nothing day.
A sleep-till-noon, don't-have-to-stop-for-homework,
play-video-games-&-eat-&-eat-&-eat day.

Mom didn't get the memo.
She hands me a list of household chores.
Chores that aren't on my paid Plant Assistant list.

Mow lawn? Trim hedges? Clean garage? Whaa?
I tell her my body needs rest for the challenges.
She laughs. *Boy, I'm helping you build stamina.*

The whole ride to the airport, Dad doesn't rescue me either.
Not one *Come on, give the boy a break* or nothing. *Nothing!*

I plead with him to take my side.
At least let me chill for an early birthday present.
He parts his lips, she cuts her eyes.
Dad says, *Do what your mother tells you.*

Chores

Yeah, I organize the garage, sweating like it's a hundred &
five degrees. I get to #6: *clean room* & faint with relief.
Air-conditioning!

I make my bed, pick dirty clothes from the floor,
put away clean ones too. Stack shoes on the rack,
pile comics back into the box.
    My comics—
I pick one up.
Man, me & Darius would flip pages all day long.

Him: *Dude, what's up with Jakeem Thunder?*
Me: *Yeah, DC know they can give bro more action.*
Him: *Yo, for real, Storm would be my girl.*
Me: *Dude, Storm? You'd have to fight T'Challa. You sure you
want that beef?*

That's us. For hours.
That *was* us. For hours.

We Do This.
The second day of summer, Drew's at my door. Stoked.
Ball tucked under his arm, cell in his hand.

Check it! He unlocks his phone. Shows me his list.
#1. Four square.
#2.
      Yo, where's the rest? I say.
Ain't gon' need no more. Bro, F-O-U-R S-Q-U-A-R-E.

I remind Drew it's only two of us.
I don't say it but think it: *Only us two.*
Now we change our game to two square.
      Yeah, it's a thing.

Quick, I check the existing record on the internet & learn two facts.
   1. The longest four square game was a marathon that lasted twenty-nine hours. Twenty-nine hours?!
   2. The rules state we need to be at least sixteen. SIXTEEN!?!

We'd have to wait two & a half more years.
We don't have two & a half years to wait.

Dang, bro. Drew rubs his head. *What you got?*

I grab my phone, show him my list.
#1. Burger eating.
#2.
    Bro, he says. *Where's your number two?*
Not gonna need it. Dude, B-U-R-G-E-R-S. You love burgers!
Drew stashes his ball, grabs his bike. *Yep, sho' do.*

World Record #1: Bubba's Burgers

We sit on a curb in Bubba's Burgers parking lot.
I'm three burgers in.
Thirteen's the record.
Which means we gotta chow fourteen.

I take a breath, hyperfocus, &
totally down my fourth.
Drew grabs his sixth. *You full yet?*
I unwrap my fifth. *Nah,* I lie.
Me neither, he says, taking a bite.

A few minutes later, the same fifth burger nudges my lips.
Jaws refuse to budge.

Dude, you still good? I groan.
I'm good. Drew sloth-slow chomps his seventh.
I don't let on that my stomach is rumbling.
Roiling.

Still I cram down the fifth, seriously regretting this challenge.
By the sixth, it's a wrap. Ready to call quits, when

my brain reminds me why I'm doing this in the first place.
My stomach ain't listening.

Dude. I gag. *Gonna . . . be sick.*
I put a fist to my mouth, afraid number five
or all six burgers'll reappear.

Drew's been holding his eighth
for the last five minutes.

This sounded easy and ho-hum, I confess.
Ain't easy. Or ho-hum. Drew leans back on the grass.
Stretches his stomach, makes room for more.
He finally lifts the burger, then drops it.
Bro, I'm out.

It's on me. Just seven more.
I   can   do   this.

I reach for another burger . . .
ignore the bubbling . . .
bite . . .
ignore the churning . . .
chew . . .
ignore the rising . . .
swallow . . .
Yes! Success!

Four minutes later, Drew is doubled over snort-laughing
as my head faces the ground introducing the earth
to the contents of my stomach.

Dude, I say, in between breaths, *I'm never gonna eat
another burger again.*
Yeah, right, says the cackling hyena. *Ain't your birthday
coming up? Yo, you getting a whole bagful.*

Nooo. I gasp as my stomach heaves.
Again. & dang, again.

World Record #1

#1. Tying knots while standing in ice water,
    aka Yo, my toes so cold! 3:54
(*Our first score!*—big up to Drew!)

Drew hovers over my shoulder as I lean
into my laptop typing in our first win &
uploading the video to the Guinness site
that proves we are champions.
He posts our video on his page. *We gon' blow up.*

Funny thing, I get a swole-chest feeling like Darius
must have had when he scored his first record—
the longest to balance a book on his head
while skateboarding. Dude wouldn't stop jumping
up & down, celebrating. Got me so excited
I wanted in too.

Just that fast, my swole chest shrinks
thinking about how we'll never do another record
with Darius again.

World Record, aka *Bro, What's Up with These Toe Challenges?*

We're outside on the porch
'cause Mom said our feet smell
was mixing with her zen smell
& it was disturbing her peace.
        Yo, my feet don't stink.

Shoes & socks off. We grasp marbles
with our *paintless* toes
until Drew gets a cramp &
we laugh so hard we sweat.
He pulls up his shirt, wipes his face.
That's when I see it. A bruise, big, on his side.
It's all purpley. *Dannggg.*
He drops his shirt. *Slap boxing with
Randy & Marcus—*
        You mean punch boxing?
Yeah, straight crushed it, he says quick,
like that was it & goes back to toe grabbing.
        Guess it is. For now.

World Record #2

#2: Dude, move those long claws out the way & let
   the master drop marbles into a bucket!

A hundred & two marbles, 2:04 (*Big up to me!*),
aka since when you start slap boxing with
Marcus & Randy?

Endangered Species

Dad's back for my birthday, and right now
he's at the table big boastin' like
he's the master of photography just because
he captured a picture of some monkey.

No no no, not just some monkey, he corrects.
The golden langur.

I study the screen. The monkey has gold halo-like fur.
Black face. Thick lips. And big round eyes that,
from Dad's pic, look like they're low-key judging.

Dad beams. *Not only is this primate sacred to the Himalayan
people but it is one of the most endangered species of India.
Look*—he zooms in on a shot—*he's yawning. Yawning!
Amazing, right?*

Yeah, amazing, I say, bored of monkey pictures.
Can we talk about my birthday now?

Dad laughs. Closes his laptop. *Yeah, of course,
my soon-to-be teen.*

Now I'm laughing. *Teen? Pfft, I'm already that.*
And there he goes, soft eyeing me with the same
my son is growing up look Mom does.
But I'm not waiting for him to say it.

So, I start. *I'm thinking red velvet cake....*
He nods for me to go on.
Oh, I will. I sit down because I'm just getting started.

Smells Like Teen Spirit

On my birthday, Drew's a no-show.
Texted something came up. What, he didn't say.

Me, Mom, and Dad crowd around the
candle*less* cake she baked with a loopy
Happy 14th Birthday Isaiah! on top.

Just two, Mom pleads, holding a pair of candles
with the numbers one and four. *Pleeease, we have to have
them.*

Last year, Darius and Drew stood on the other side
of the table ripping jokes—*Don't spit on the cake!*

I say yes to the candles. She lights them. I blow them out.
For her. She thanks me with smothering kisses until I squirm.
Mom! She throws her head back laughing and wipes
lipstick off my cheeks.

Mom cuts the cake. Three slices. Slides me the biggest.

Last year, Darius and Drew inhaled the cake like
it was *their* birthdays.

What's wrong? she asks. *You're not hungry?*
I take a bite.

Dad drops gift bags onto the table.
You know what time it is.

I tear into a card from Uncle Vent and Aunt Terri.
Fifty dollars. Nice.

Dad gives me a black-and-red Santa Cruz—*Yes!*—skateboard
designed with a big blue hand and right in the center of its
palm is a wide-open mega mouth. *Dooope! Thanks, Dad.*
He winks at Mom like he beat her at gift giving.

From Mom—*A David Bowie concert tee!* Bowie's on the
front, leaning back with guitar raised, rocking. *Whoa whoa
whoa, this is awesome, Mom. Thanks!*

It's a 1987, see. She points to the concert dates.
Then she winks back at Dad.

He folds his arms and frowns like his feelings are hurt.
Dad, thank you. This skateboard is legit dope, for real.
He smugly smiles at Mom.

As soon as the sun goes down,
I dip out the house
stare up the street to nothing
lie on Mom's car hood
gaze at the sky
and think of a wish to make.

Would Could Should

The next morning,
Dad's on the floor in the living room.
A contact sheet of small black-and-white rectangles
in his hand. Magnifying glass to his eye.
A carpetful of photos spread out in front of him.

You know, I should make a book like Gordon Parks.
Better yet, I could present in a gallery like Carrie Mae Weems. . . .
If I could, I'd put on an expo like W. E .B. DuBois. . . .
Or just set up my own studio like James Van Der Zee.

You know, I should. . . .
Better yet, I could. . . .
If I could, I would. . . .
Or just . . .

Like Eli Reed . . . like Jeanne Moutoussamy-Ashe . . .
like P. H. Polk . . .
Like . . .
Like . . .
Like . . .

Dad's dreams float above his head, showcasing him in a
gallery, then in a studio with his art book on a table.
He looks up as if deciding which one to catch.

I wish I could plant my own *shoulds* in Dad's head
so he could picture his dream to be back here with me.
With us.

At least he's here now, I tell myself. Drew's birthday is in
three weeks, and his dad can't come home for it.
Wait, what if *that's* why something mysteriously came up
yesterday?

It'd suck for Drew, hanging out here
when on his own birthday, he'll be dad*less*.

I sidle down next to Dad, okay with knowing he can at least
come home . . . and does.

Then I remember . . . a while back, Mom told
Uncle Vent and Aunt Terri something about
Dad's work contract. So I ask him about it.

He tells me that yeah, his contract will expire in
August, and they've already offered him another year.

Another year?

Dad stops his picture sorting.
I love what I've done, love what I've seen.
'Saiah, the world is so big.

Yeah, I say, *but it's small too.*
I hope, really hope he hears how much I miss him.

Dad picks up a black-and-white photo of me and Mom bent over a peace lily. I was like, five? Never seen this pic before.

He stares at the photo for the longest.
Then finally *finally* says, *Yeah, I think it's time for me to come home.*

The New Trio

I take my new board out for a spin.
Up my block, around my corner,
past the school,
which is totally empty,
to the skate park,
that's totally packed.
On my way home,
halfway up the block
at the corner of Sycamore Street
sitting on bikes
are Marcus & Randy.
I debate keeping straight,
or taking a detour,
when I spot Drew,
who was MIA yesterday.
Even though I got questions,
suddenly I ain't in the mood to get into
the what's & whys & how comes.
Guess, there's nothing for me to do but
hit a left & skate that way.

World Record Epic Fails

- Can't chew fast enough to eat fifty donut holes in a minute, aka Bruh, after Bubba's Burgers, why? aka Don't worry about it, we got the next one.

- Watch-movies-till-movies-watch-us martial arts movie marathon, aka Dude, before you say *The Last Dragon*, we going with never-seen-befores, aka Why you hatin' on my movie? aka Are you even trying to stay awake?

- Dude, this is the stupidest idea lifting heavy rocks over our heads aka then you come up with a better idea aka the records thing was your idea aka if you didn't want to do it then you should've said so aka I did want to, you know what, forget it, what's next?

Paper Airplanes

The wind blew us into my room.
Socks & jeans are strewn across the floor like seaweed.
I hurry to pick them up. *My bad.*

Drew smirks. *You should see mine. Yo,*
it's mad weird being in here during the day.
He stares at the posters over my bed.
LeBron James. Stephen Curry. Kobe Bryant, RIP.
I ain't know you like basketball like that.

Dad got me those posters, & nah, I don't like basketball like that.
Can't play, even though everybody thinks it 'cause I'm tall.

Drew goes to my window. Picks up a baby rubber tree.
Yo, you really are a flower boy.
Bruh, it's a plant. Now you sound like Marcus and Randy.

Drew jokes, *Bet you be talking to it.* He smooches and coos,
Hey, baby.
Bruh. Seriously? Yeah, okay okay, I do talk to plants.
They like that sorta stuff. They're living.

I hand Drew half a stack of copy paper.
He plops down at my desk.
I set out a box to land the planes into, then settle
at the edge of my bed with the other half of the paper.

He folds a sheet, creases. Starts up about Vanessa.
How she thought our tie-in-ice record was hilarious.

You show her our stunts?
Drew flies his plane. It lands. *She follows me.*
He pulls up his page. *We getting some likes.*

We fold, crease, & fly.
Some land. Some don't.

After a while he says, *Aye, how much money you think
people win for breaking records?*
Nothing. I fold a piece in half. *Honor. Maybe.*

Honor? Drew flies another plane. It lands. Again.
I need more than that.
I fold over the wings. *Maybe endorsement deals?
Talk shows? Why?*

Drew rubs his thumb over a scuff on his sneaks.
What you'd do if you had a million dollars?
He doesn't answer my *why*. I fly my plane. It misses.
Dag. I don't know.

You oun't know? Yo, you don't dream 'bout money?
I mean, not really, I tell him.
His dark eyes sweep over my room. *Pfft, I do.*

There he goes, getting all mum again. A few minutes later,
he stands. Stretches. *Bro, I'm outta paper.*

I point to another stack on the floor outside my closet door,
now figuring what I'd do with a million bucks.
Buy my own jet? Go to every concert—

Yooo, nice. My skateboard. Drew runs his hand over
the top. *When you get this?*
My birthday. I crease another sheet.

Cyborg? He picks up a comic. *Bro, don't tell me you
still read these.*
I used to—Whoa.
                    Wait.
                              My comics.
                                        My closet!
                                                    My—
I jump up. Paper spills to the floor. *Hold up*—

What th—Drew pushes my clothes to the side.
He takes in each & every poster.
Metallica. AC/DC.
Queen. Oxymorrons.

Wannabe-white-boy-rock-star rushes my ears.
He turns to me. *Yo, what's all this?*

I start to lie. But he stares at the walls.
Then the comics.   Then the plants.
Then my shoes.   & back to the walls.

Now I look too. See what he sees.
My box of comics.   The succulents.
Vans and Chucks.   Rock posters.

Part of me is relieved, so freakin' relieved he knows.
Maybe I can stop hiding. Hiding me.
But no. How would I look admitting
I like paint on my toes, banging to punk rock,
collecting vintage tees, & yeah, even talking to plants—

Drew points to the closet. *Gotta admit, that's mad weird.*
He rubs his head. *I oun't get it, yo.*

See, this is what I'm talking about. Now I'm wanting
to explain how I didn't want him or Darius to think
I was some cornball. But I couldn't say that. You know
how much of a cornball I'd really sound like?

But now, what pops out of my mouth is stupid. Just dumb.
What pops out is *I don't get why you come at night.* But I
don't say nothing.

Bro, don't do that. He takes a breath. An impatient breath.
Don't be tantrum petty. He tosses the paper onto the desk,
starts folding again.

Tantrum petty?
Sounds just like *We can't be acting like li'l kids*.
Dag. Got me suddenly feeling like one too.

World Records #3, #4, #5
We stare at the box on the floor in the middle of
the living room.
Neither me or he mention yesterday. Not a word.
But it's there. Simmering under our skin
like his purpley punching-game bruises,
his late-night visits, & not talking about Darius.

Drew walks around the planes. *How many we got?*
Three hundred.
He goes through the challenges. *First, we'll try to land all three hunned—*
Hundred, Mom corrects with a smile. She sits on the chaise & eats popcorn like she's at AMC.

Hundred, repeats Drew with a sigh. *Then we gon' try to get three hundred*—he looks to Mom—*blindfolded. Then with rubber gloves.*

We do thirty minutes of practice rounds. Then start.
I fly, Drew flies. I fly, Drew flies.
Mom is quiet like she's at Wimbledon.
Feels intense, like we're there too.
Eyes open: 264

Neither of us cheers the other on.
We scowl as we aim & scoff when one misses.

Blindfold. I fly, Drew flies. I fly, Drew flies.
Dang. Dog.
I fly, Drew flies.
Blindfolded: 128

Slowly we loosen what we both got wrapped inside.
Slowly give props.

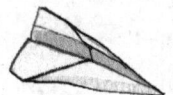

Brush it off, you good.
Told you we got this!
Soon, we're clowning each other for missing.
Soon, we're gloating when we don't.

Rubber gloves. I fly, Drew flies. I fly, Drew flies.
We stifle back laughter. Our planes are off by miles.
Bro, let me drizzle my secret sauce.
Rubber-gloved: 203
Yeah, boy! Told you I'm nice wit it!

We blow the first by twelve. Twelve!
We can't go out like this, Drew says.
We go again.

We stretch like yoga masters.
We're pumped like WWE wrestlers.
I fly, Drew flies. Again. Again. And again.
279!

What! Give me some! I thrust out my hand.
Drew slides out his too.
We front hand slap, back hand slap, dap, dap, palm clasp.
We let go, realizing at the same time
we haven't done our shake since . . . before.

We stand in a trance
when Mom breaks the spell—
    So, what's next?

What's Next?
We crouch in a tree's shade near the curb at
Drew's apartment's parking lot. We break down &
rebuild our bikes. Our fingertips dark & greasy.
We're both mummy silent when out of the blue Drew says,
Think this gon' be my last one.
Me: *What you mean?*
He: *Things getting kinda busy for me.*

Wu-Tang Clan raps from his cell.
"Cash rules everything around me. . . ."
His dad's favorite. Said his dad digs their buttery, grimy rhymes.
Drew nods as he mumbles the lyrics.
My rock stays locked in my phone.

Me: *Busy . . . 'cause of the other day?*
He: *Nah . . . just got stuff going on.*

Drew lifts his back wheel, rotates the crank.
The chain loops onto the disc.
His phone chimes. Again.
He rubs his oiled fingertips on
an old T-shirt we use as a rag.

He checks the message,
laughs, & mutters, *He stupid.*

I'm guessing *he* is either Marcus or Randy.
Who may be stupid. But aren't . . . weird.

So that's it? I say. *You quitting just like that?*
Drew rubs his forehead with the back of his hand.
You even know why I said yeah to this?

I think back to the day in the media center. *'Cause of Vanessa.
At first.* He picks up the pliers. *But now I need money. Real
money. And ain't too much I can do to make it, legally.*

Why? But then I spy his shoes. Deep creases cross the toes.
For new kicks?
Drew sneers. *Yeah sure, for sneaks. And this* ain't *getting
enough likes to get 'em.*

But we weren't doing this for likes.
You weren't, he corrects. *'Sides, I don't know why you
wanna do these records anyway.*

Why Am *I* Doing This?

The records were our new wild stuff,
even though it would never replace our old wild stuff
like trying on Jays with no money
like skidding out at the skate park
like jumping off roofs.
But that's not why I wanted to do the records.
Not at first.

I wanted Drew to open up. *I* wanted to open up.
To joke about stuff, like me sliding down that mountain.
Darius wiping out & him mad grinning with his head dizzy
with stars. Talking about it was bananas. *Bananas.*

What's so funny? Drew cuts off my thoughts.
I didn't realize I was laughing. He asked, so I spill it. *And Bro
tore his bike up. Was ready to go again like it was nothing.*

Shockingly, Drew smirks.
I go on. *Had us poppin' wheelies till my arms gave out.*
Drew grins.

He doesn't shut down & I explode & talk about—
Darius getting chased by a boxer 'cause he swore
he was a dog whisperer.
Him almost breaking his leg 'cause he swore
he could backflip off a brick wall.
Him soaring off my garage 'cause he watched
Miles Morales & bet he could land just like him.
Talk about . . .
Talk about . . .
Maannn, just talk . . .

Wanna know why I want to do the records?
Like Drew, my *why* changed. I know now that
it's not something me & Drew have to do.
Not for us, but—
for Darius.

Drew holds his tongue, so I press on.
Dude, don't you see we gotta do what he *didn't finish.*
Drew watches a car parking.
And, I add, *you could post it. Should post it. For him.*

Drew's foot taps. Small eyes turn to slits.
Swear he's in a sleeping bag about to zip himself up.
Swear he's regretting our whole mission.
Swear I'm about to crush under his silence when
he finally says, *Okay. The wheelie. For Darius.*
Yeah, I say. *Cool,* the wheelie.

And—he pauses—*the mountain too.*

A baseball lump clogs my throat. *The . . . mountain?*
Yep. & with straight fire in his voice, he says, *We promised.*

I wipe my brow.
Aight, bet. The mountain too.

Something Else Too

Deep inside, it feels like there's something
I need to do. For Darius. Alone.
Yeah, okay, sounds weird, but it's like
his spirit won't rest until I do it.
That's why I keep coming here. To Rosewood.

I've got to pop a wheelie. On this street.
Can't be scared. Can't flake.

I'm supposed to meet Drew, but
I'm here, at the corner, facing the past.
That *day* rushes me. I wrestle it back.
All the way back to us rock paper scissors–ing.
I stand here at this corner, until
I'm ready. Finally, finally ready.

I pedal forward	forward	forward
until I reach	*the*	place

where we three front hand slapped & palm clasped.
Where I said my last words to him. *Be like water.*
He said his last to me. *Always.*

Two little girls play outside in a yard.
A cat in a window, watches.
No cars. No Yelling Man.

For Darius, I whisper.
I tighten my backpack.
Ride down to the cul-de-sac. Take my start.
One two three—I go.
Gain speed & pop.
Hold it! Hold it!
I near the corner.
Ears tuned for an engine's roar.
None. I keep popping!

I make it over, circle back around.
Gripping the handlebars. Straining my arms.
Don't see the girls playing or the cat watching.
Don't see the lawn statues or the birdbaths.
Don't see nothing but my goal.

Focus, balance, hold it. Hold it. Hold it.
I reach, at last, to the other end—yes!—& drop the wheel.
I did it. *I freakin' did it!*
Not three minutes for the record.
But down Rosewood. For Darius!
I didn't choke. I didn't quit.
I. Did. It.

I pump the air with my fist.
Heart on supercharge.
I grab my water bottle from my backpack.
Take a gulp.
Glance around—no one's watching—
& pour some on the ground.

  For my homie, I say, like they do in the movies.
   The GOAT of—

Hey! You Lost?!
The man, same man, is on his porch.   *This dude!*
He calls to me. I don't answer.   *Why can't I answer?!*
He steps toward the street. I turn my bike to flee.
But no, I can't
        don't
                WON'T.

Hey, what're you doing?
He's getting close. His face is bottled fury.
I can't stay. Should stay. Will stay.
But like a mouse I
           scurry
                away.

                No.
           No!
       NO!
I stand my ground. Glare him down.
A flicker in his eyes. His sight darts to the spot.
He remembers.
Remembers yelling, pointing, shoving.

Remembers the chaos, the car braking too late.
Remembers me, Drew, Darius.
He remembers that day. *That* day!
I know he does!
He opens his mouth—

But I don't wanna hear sorry, or that it was a mistake.
Because there's nothing—*nothing*—he could say that'll
make it all okay.

He should know if it wasn't for him
Drew would've finished recording the time
I would've seen that car
Darius would've broken a record—
would be alive to break more!

I gotta get the words out or I'll explode.
I unstick my lips and I
yell,
        yell,
                YELL!

BECAUSE OF YOU MY FRIEND IS DEAD!

The man's face drops.
            He frowns.
                      Then scowls.
The rage is back.
            He charges. At me.
                      I bike away. Fast.

Straight to Meet Drew

I'm behind the skate park. Drew's not here.
I text: *wya*
My heart still races. Legs still pumped.

Calm down, I tell myself.
I laugh a little. I *did* it.
I rode down Rosewood. Yelled back at the man too.

Earbuds rock Kravitz.
I squat close to the ground. Wait for Drew.

I toss a handful of pebbles into the air.
They fall like rain. *Plat, plat, plat.*
I check my phone.
Where is he? Should charge bro a late fee.

My heart calms. Kravitz's guitar screams.
Don't hear the crunching. Soles on rocks.
But my eyes rise in time to see

    two men blasting fast
    like balls from a cannon.
    The target is me—

Done

Don't see clouds.
Don't feel the sun.
Don't hear the birds chirp or motors hum.
Don't feel my feet shuffle one in front of the other.

She sees me before I see her. *Mom.*
At the mailbox. Mail in hand.
Her mouth moves but her syllables are blocked
by the pounding in my ears.

You're limping. You fall, honey?
One of those crazy stunts?
I hear, but don't.
My mind is left back at the lot.

Where you been? Isaiah, why're you bleeding?
She drops the envelopes. Snatches my face,
turns it left, right. *You fall?* she asks again.
No, I mumble.

She fingers the rip in my shirt,
the dirt on my jeans.

Her eyes bulge wild.
Isaiah, what happened?

I squeeze my handlebars. Tight.
Mom's almost shouting:
Talk to me! What happened?

Nothinnnnng. I break away.
My chest hurts, shoulder's jacked,
knuckles scratched.

The left side of my face burns.
My mouth swollen with anger.
Wants to breathe out dragon fire.

I clench my teeth, bite my roar
back back back.
Isaiah, please? She begs now. *Tell me—*
Mom, I say, strong. Final. *I'm fine.*

Mom Frets

Mom frets about me
So how can I tell her as
she waits for an answer while
rubbing ointment over open wounds while
more questions build on her tongue as
she worries about lasting scars?

Panic Calls

Mom calls Dad. Over and over.
Curses because he's somewhere unreachable.
Amazon rainforest? Down Under? Alaska?
She slams her phone on the table hard enough to crack
the screen. *Why won't the call go through?*

She runs her hands through her hair.
I'll call your uncle Vent.
I go to my bedroom. Close the door.
Pace around. And around.
Spot my beanie on the shelf.
Grab it. Yank it on my head.

Mom bursts in. Sees my hat.
Hand flies to her mouth.
Your uncle wants to talk to you.
She holds out the phone. I take it.

Don't have a choice.

Blink

Uncle Vent says, *This your uncle*, like I don't know.
He asks how things are and if everything's good.
I blink away the men. Blink away the hands. I blink.
Uncle Vent, I sigh. *It was a little scuffle, that's all.*

He *mmm-hmmms*.
      You'd run home to tell your mom about a fight?
Hmmm. Probably nodding and rubbing his chin.
Just boys fighting?
      Yeah, just boys fighting.
And you're okay?
      Nothing's broken, I say.

He tells me to call if I wanna talk.
I tell him, *I will.*

I hang up and blink this all away.

The Day-After Text

Drew: *meet at the spot at noon*
Me: *where were you yesterday*

My phone screen is cracked,
fractures spread like spiderwebs.
I can see enough to ignore
Drew's *my bad* response.

The Day After, Mom

Instead of TV, Mom watches me close.
Her sight blind to *The View*.

Isaiah, you want to talk, she says, *about anything?*
    Nope.
You sure?
    Yeah, I'm sure. I hug her. *Thought Uncle Vent filled*
    you in.
She sucks her breath. *He only told me not to worry.*

    I get a Pop-Tart. *And you won't listen to your big brother?*
    I go outside, grab my bike.
Mom follows me down the walk. *Isaiah, think you can help*
divide these hostas?
    Mom.
Okay, okay. Answer your phone when I call you.

I go up the block.
At the corner, I peek back.
She's still there.

Text
Drew: *yo, wya?*
Me:

Now Dad

So, you had a fight, huh?
Dad asks if I want to talk about it.
I tell him I just wanna drop it.

He asks if it was with Drew.
I tell him, *No*, then switch the subject to our new mission.

Oh, he says. *Like, in honor of Darius. That's nice, 'Saiah.*
But just like Mom, he's back fretting. *Do I need to come home?*

I've been wanting him home since he left.
But a voice in my head whispers, *Gotta be toughened up.*

Naw, a few hands thrown. That's all.
He repeats, *And that's all?*
Yep, that's all.

Yeah okay, that's *not* all.
But if I keep saying that,
then maybe it'll feel true.

Back to Drew

Drew finds me in the library.
Immersed in the Spider-Verse.
He slinks into a chair.
I turn down my music.

Bruh, went looking for you.
Out of all places, you in the library?
The library, yo?
His eyes already down on his phone.

Yeah, bro, needed to look somethin' up right quick.
I flip
flip
flip
through page
after page.

Bruh, why you ain't show? Don't tell me 'cause of yesterday.
That'd be mad flakey.
      Flakey? I spit. *I'd be mad flakey?*
Drew finally looks up. *Dag, dude, what happened to yo' face?*

What happened. Pfft. He wasn't there, that's what
happened. Part of me wants to say that *and* more.
Blame him because if he'd said he wasn't gon' come,
I would've went home. Or, if he'd shown, this might not've
happened. Not with both of us there.

And still, there's the other part of me, who wants
to get it out, tell him the facts. Blow by blow.
But now, with whichever Drew—old or new—
sitting across from me, nah, I'm good.

Well? he says.
    Fell off my skateboard.
Dang, bro, you really took a hit.

Hit. Hits.

I close the comic book.
My hands tremble.
Yep. I did.

Nightly News

I chill with Mom while
she watches the nightly news
There's a lot to cover, the man says
a bombing overseas
a mass shooting over there
a protest over here
suddenly
the newscaster's face is the man's face
his hands are the men's hands and they
s   t   r   e   t   c   h
from the screen and
r   e   a   c   h
inside my chest and
s   q   u   e   e   z   e
and
s   q   u   e   e   z   e
until Mom lowers the volume
Are you okay?

Yeah, yeah, I'm fine, I say,
and bolt before she gets to asking more.

At Night I'm a Hurricane
ripping posters off the walls
shoving stuff off my dresser
yanking clothes from my closet.

I'm fine!

I'm a rocker raging and screaming
all the words I wanted to say but couldn't.

I'm fine!

In my dream, Darius lies on the ground.
His eyes blank. Mouth opens to speak.
Nothing comes out.

I'm fine!

The men wake me from my sleep
drag me from bed by my feet
trample my spine
my screams stay trapped
in my throat
I curl up
panting like a dog
whimpering,

I'm fine. I'm fine. I'm fine.

Mom

I eat a turkey sandwich with cheese.
Mom sips tea. Glances at her hanging pothos,
the hat on my head, my bruised face.

Isaiah, you never told me about the other day.
I'll leave it alone if you want.
Okay, I say.

I climb my bike.
She stands on the porch.
The ferns are looking pretty thirsty.

I plug my earbuds in. Ride down the block.
At the corner I don't look back.
But know for sure she's still there.

We Poppin' Wheelies

Drew doesn't get why we're in his parking lot.
Too many cars come through here, yo.

Cars fill the spaces like a half-toothless mouth.
We ride up and down, pausing for each vehicle.

Sweat dribbles down the sides of my face.
But I keep my beanie on.

Drew takes off to the left. I dip to the right.
I flip up my front tire, warm my muscles.
Count the seconds. *Six. Seven. Eight. Nine . . .*

Aye, watch out! calls Drew.
A horn blow. I swerve.
A Honda passes.

He rides up. *That was close.*
Too close. Could've gotten hit. Could've been worse—

Yo, this ain't gon' work. Drew says we ain't gotta go to
Rosewood, but we're going to a street over there with

a cul-de-sac. *You said you wanted to do what Darius couldn't, didn't you?*

My body pulses. Sends all kinds of alarms. Or fear.
Drew stares at me like a watchdog.
Stares like I'm gonna flake.

Fine. Let's go.

Greenlake Lane

We're two streets over from Rosewood.
Cedar cuts through it.

I am timer, video recorder, and watcher.
Hand ready to steady the phone
so he can post a tribute online.

We take a moment of silence.   For Darius.
Drew rides down to the end of Greenlake's cul-de-sac.

I post at the corner.
A minute later he takes off.
I press record. Hands already sweaty.
                                       Drew pops his tire.
I hit the timer. Heart hammering.
Hands soggy sweating.
                                       He's popping.

I'm watching. For cars. The man. The men. Those two men.
Fifty-seconds! I yell. *You got this!*

He's near the other end.
A truck. A white truck. Is two streets away.
Two streets away is Rosewood Lane.
Rosewood Lane is two streets away.

And that day—*that* day barges in. Bullies me.
Asks why couldn't I call *car* that day?
Why my throat locked tight and tongue shriveled up that day?
Why I didn't yell back like Drew that day?
Why wasn't I tough enough to say anything that day?
If I had, it would've went differently that day.
                                Drew's at the other end. Circling.

Be like water, that's what I said to Darius. Our saying.
Always. That's what he said back to me. Our answer.
Always means forever.
Forever and ever.
Eternity. Infinity.
And now—now always means
at no time,
not ever,
nevermore.
Means there'll never ever be another day with Darius.
Because of me.

The truck. The truck is one block away.
One block past Rosewood Lane.
                                Drew's coming back up the street.

I didn't yell that day because *I* choked.
I choke every single time.
Every single time, I choke.
Can't stop either.
Can't even tell Mom and Dad the truth about what happened.
Because . . . because I freakin' choke.
God, what is wrong with me?

                                  Drew's near Cedar!

The truck's near Greenlake!
My breathing. So fast.
Hands. So clammy.
Chest. So tight.
I push,
I fight
fight with all my might
to push the boulder
that blocks my throat.
For Darius. For Drew. For Drew. For Darius.
I yell, finally—
CARRR!

Panic

Drew slams into a parked car.
I wanna see if he's okay.
But I can't move. It's like my feet,
my feet are stuck in a barrel of cement and
I'm tipping, tipping off a pier to the sea below.

Drew gets up. His bike left on the ground.
He rushes me. I stumble.

What's the matter with you? he shouts. *I know you saw it!*
I can't tell him. Tell him I almost choked. Again.
But I yelled, I say. I yelled car. I did, finally.
Yeah, almost too late. He rubs his shoulder. *Coulda got hit.*
Hit, yo, and you, you *supposed to have my back.* . . .

Blood crashes through my eardrums loud like ocean waves
and in that moment, that moment
what I hear is: *You didn't have Darius's back!*
What I hear is: *It's your fault he got hit!*
What I hear is: *Now he's gone.*

And it's true. It's all true.
And it hurts. Hurts bad.
And I attack. Attack fast.

You blame me. For Darius. I knew it.
What? He throws up his hands. *Bro, what're you talking about?*

I'm talking about months of stuff that's been bottled inside.
And I burst. I burst.

Me: *You blame me. That's why you shut me out!*
Drew: *What? Dude, everything ain't about you.*
Me: *I know but that's the reason. Ain't it?*

Drew: *Yo, what you want? Want me to pat yo' back 'cause you feel guilty? Tell you it's okay?*—He waves me off.—*Bro, get outta here wit' that.*

Me: *Then why does it seem like I'm the only one who thinks about him? Only one replaying that day in my mind?*

Drew: *Dude, you ever slow down your me, me, me to wonder how I might feel?*—He jabs his chest.—*I watched him die too!*—He jabs harder.—*You don't think I go over in my mind what I could've done to save him? Got my own regrets, yo. Ain't nobody got time for yours too.*

Me: *But for the longest you ain't have nothing to say about Darius. He was our boy. Our boy—*

Drew: *Bro, you don't get it. I ain't got time to keep talking about who ain't here when I gotta focus on who is. Got my brother in and out the hospital. My mom trying to hold it down. And my dad—*(he stops.)

Me: *Yeah, I know he's in the army. I get it but—*
Drew (goes for his bike): *You don't know nothing.*
Me: *I know enough.*
Drew:
Me: *See, there you go again. Shutting down.*
Drew: *Since you just gotta know everything—everything—*
Me (heart thumping fast):
Drew: *My dad's in jail. Happy now?*

Me: *Jail? Since when? Why? What he do?*
Drew: *Wha—what you say?*
Me: *Nah. That's not what I—*

Drew throws down his bike, rushes me for the second time.
His face close. So close to mine. *Bro . . . I swear . . .*
His chest heaves. Heaves hard and fast. Fists ball.
You must be trippin' sayin' something like that to me.

*Wait, I didn't . . . I—*I stammer—
Yo, get out of my face, Isaiah. Better get the hell on.

I'm Fine

I open the door. Slam it shut.
Mom asks what happened.
I tell her, *Nothing*.

Isaiah, I wish you'd talk to me. You sure—
        How many times I gotta say I'm fine? Dang.
I'm sorry, she apologizes. *I'm just . . . You're just—*

I can't help it.
I shout
one   last   time—
I'm FINE!
I'M FINE!
Wish you would stop asking because
I
AM
FINE!

Feeling Like Straight Landfill

Mom got Dad ringing my phone again.
Before he begins, I start.
I tell him I said something foul to Drew.
He asks if it's so foul I can't fix.
I say, *Might be.*

Dad asks if I'm *sure* I'm okay.
I tell him I'm sure.

He tells me Mom worries about me.
I'm good—
Afraid I'll get into trouble with the fighting.
I'm not—
That it'll be a good idea to spend the rest of the summer with him in Alaska.
Alaska?
Photographing glaciers.
Glaciers?

No way I'm going to Alaska.
I've got thin blood. *Thin blood!*
Naw, I say. *I'm straight.*

He tells me their minds are made up.
If you're not here with me—he pauses—*then you'll be going to North Carolina with your uncle and aunt.*

North Carolina?
Sorry, he sighs.

Sorry for them.
'Cause I ain't going nowhere.

When Plants Are Not Enough

On the worktable is a round glass bowl.
Mom places a succulent inside it, delicately.

She says she's afraid I'm going down the wrong path.
She wants me to talk to her. Give her something.
But if I talk, I'll make it real. And if it's real, then . . .

Then this vacation will do you good. She cocks her head,
deciding which plants to add to the terrarium.

You'll make friends. She pushes a square bowl
in front of me.

I don't touch it.

You are so much like your father. Mom places a purplish
succulent next to a green one. *He got moody. Easily irritated.
Sat for hours watching the news.*

Okay yeah, before Dad started at *National Geo*, he was
kinda quiet at times. Kinda crabby too.

She hands me a tiny cactus. *That's when I knew he needed a change.*

I put the cactus on the table. *He left.*

Mom picks the plant back up. *And he's coming back. Soon.* She hands it to me again. *You'll leave. And come back soon too.*

Quiet Rage

Three days later,
Uncle Vent finds me out back twirling nunchucks.
He looks at me with the same light brown face as Mom's.
Same curly hair, except short, and more salt than pepper.

He tells me Mom doesn't know what to do with my daytime
busyness, nighttime pacing, or quiet rage.

I flip my chucks over my shoulder, catch the bottom under
my right pit. *I don't have no rage.*

He tells me a change of scenery might do me good.
Flip, catch, flip, catch. Exactly what they said too.

Maybe they're wrong.
Might be right.
Nothing makes sense anymore.
My mind is stuck on pause.
Can't move forward or reverse.

Goodbye

Mom hugs me.
My arms stay limp at my side. *Why I gotta go?*
She squeezes me.
Why can't I stay here? Mom, pleeease . . .
She rubs a hand over my beanie.
You need this, trust me.

Before I know it, I'm begging not to be sent away.
Before I know it, my voice is cracking.
Before I know it, my eyes get watery.
But I won't cry.

Uncle Vent's at the truck, watching.
I fix my T-shirt. Turn to go.

Wait. Mom gives me one more hug.
To Uncle Vent says, *Take care of my baby.*

I ain't no baby, I say to her.
You're my baby, she says back.

From Here to There

My eyes can't stay open.
By the time I wake, we're nearly there.
I wipe crust from my corners.
Stare out the window.

Blues music plays through the speakers.
Uncle Vent's fingers tap the steering wheel like a drum.
He nods to a cooler. *Wanna drink?*
I reach in. Grab a Coke. Pop the top. Gulp.

Mom said I drank so much from the cup of anger
I'd explode with one more sip.
Seems like no matter how much I drink,
my throat still burns.

We pass drugstores, cleaners, antiques shops.
We cross train tracks and enter a whole other part of town.
Trailer parks. Mobile homes.
Cows, horses, some grazing in front yards too.
Drew would never believe this.

Drew.
Dag.

Should I text him?
Tell him I'll be away?

Better get the hell on.
Nah.

Dad told me to give him time.
Think I need it more.

Aunt Terri

Uncle Vent turns into a long drive. Pulls up behind a boat.
As soon as he puts the gear in park, Aunt Terri's stepping out
the house.

She's how I remember. Skin dark like earth. Like she was
plucked right out the ground. She's smiling mad big too.
Aunt Terri's pretty for, you know, an aunt.

We hop out the truck.
I barely stretch my legs before she's grabbing me with thick,
strong arms. *Isaiah!*

She takes my elbow. *Let me show you around.*
Uncle Vent tells her to let the boy breathe.
Aunt Terri ignores him and leads the way.

We round the side of the house to the back.
A leaning barn not ready to give up or give in
stubbornly sits in the distance.

You'll find me here most days. Aunt Terri points to a garden
with a pea-green shed to the left. *And that's your uncle's*

shed over there. She points to a little brown building.
Got all his tools and stuff.

She stands flamingo still. *Listen.*
Aunt Terri closes her eyes. *Hear that?*

It's quiet.
But then I hear it—the humming.

Growing grass, ants, slugs, spiders, fleas.
Tomatoes, peppers, okra, green beans.
All humming.

My fingertips meet the ground and dig.
Hum. Buzz.

Their land stretches long and wide.
Flat green earth carpets each direction.
With humming and buzzing all around.

The First Night

Salt, onions, and some *makes my mouth drool* seasonings
all find a home in Aunt Terri's kitchen.
They waft from pans, jars, containers, cabinets.

When my feet step into the room,
first question she asks is *You hungry?*

My stomach speaks for me.
Aunt Terri makes me a big plate of smell-good.

Fried chicken, collard greens, rice, gravy, sweet rolls.
I wipe the plate with my bread. Aunt Terri rests her hand
over mine. *Honey, let's just get you seconds.*
Uncle Vent chuckles.

I can't help it. But
this is nothing like Mom's black-bean-meat meals.

Sleep

I sleep in the first day. Second too.
Don't mean to. Just do.

I go out back, play my Switch.
Or stay in the room, play it there.

On the dresser is a black-and-white photo of
my grandma and grandpa posing by the barn.
Grandpa Alfonzo's tall. Grandma Eula's small.
Besides that, there's nothing else to look at in here.

The third day, I don't sleep in.
I go to Aunt Terri's garden and pull weeds.

She smiles. *Thank you.*
Been meaning to get to 'em.

It's only around nine o'clock.
My jeans already too hot.

Ain't No Small Garden

Think Aunt Terri's confused.
Her garden is a farm.
I follow her down rows and rows of
sweet potatoes, onions, okra, peppers,
cabbages, collards, kale, cucumbers, tomatoes,
basil, eggplant, carrots, rosemary, blueberries, strawberries.
Black-eyed Susans, peonies, and purple coneflowers too.
Some in the ground. Some in raised beds.
This *ain't* no small garden.

Aunt Terri pinches off a blueberry. *Try one.*
I pick a berry. Hesitate.
You don't have to wash it. You'll live. She smiles.

We go to the shed. *Took me some learnin' to figure out which foods grow best in light, and which in shade. What to plant with what, like basil helps tomatoes. It's a lot of care. A lot of love. And a lot of work.*

She hands me a hoe. *Ready to get dirty?*

Not in Michigan No More

After two days of hoeing and digging,
pulling and stacking, my back and arms
are grateful when Aunt Terri says, *Let's take a ride.*

We bump down the road, the truck bed loaded with
vegetables, herbs, and fruit. We park in a lot and
transport the food to a stand at the farmers market

where people sell honey and candles, body butter and pies,
corn and dried meat, flowers and syrups, apples and
pumpkins, cider and donuts—my head swivels left
and right just to see it all, and I legit get dizzy.

Aunt Terri sets up shop. Customers who seem more like
friends fill their bags as she asks about their family, their
health, and their jobs. She introduces me and they ask how
I like it here, like gardening, and the heat.

I shrug and politely smile as I silently count down the days
till I'm back home.

Grady

I try to catch a breeze in the shade on the porch swing.
Uncle Vent's in the yard fiddling with his lawn mower.

My thumbs work the controls of my Switch when this kid
comes from around back, kicking up dust.

He's gotta be about nine or ten, yardstick thin,
one hand tugging at his jeans. Other at a red wagon
stacked with boxes that're packed full of vegetables.

'Bout to take out Aunt Terri's deliveries, he says
to Uncle Vent while peeking at me.
Okay, Grady, my uncle tells him.

Hey, this Grady kid says to me. *Why you just sittin' there?*
I don't answer.
He asks my uncle why I won't talk.

Well, Grady, I suppose he'll talk when he got something to say.
My uncle glances up from the lawn mower.
Ain't that right, Isaiah?

Grady: *He wanna go for a walk, ya think?*

—Uncle Vent wipes his hands on a rag.—

Uncle Vent: *Why don't you ask him yourself?*

Grady: *'Cause . . . he'ont talk.*

Uncle Vent: *Just 'cause he don't say much don't mean he can't communicate.*

—Grady scratches his head, then gives me a half wave.—

Grady: *Hey.*

—Uncle Vent grins.—

Uncle Vent: *Don't tell me you getting shy, Grady.*

Grady: *Naw, I ain't. Wanna. Go. Walking?*

—Grady enunciates each word slow and loud.—

Uncle Vent: *Grady, he ain't deaf. Just talk normal, man.*

—This kid. I can't take no more.—

Me: *Where to?*

Umpteen Questions

Grady pulls the wagon down the drive and onto the road. He squints at me. *Ever have a girlfriend? I did. Kissed her twice. No, three times. You kissed one befo'? There're lots of girls round here. Cute ones, ugly ones, in-between ones, tall ones, short ones. They'll like you. You quiet. Girls like to talk a lot.*

I doubt how much Grady knows about girls and if he really had a girlfriend, kissed her twice, no, three times. And if he's ever been quiet long enough to listen to one to know if they like to talk a lot or not.

What happened to yo' face? You get inna a fight? You tryna hide it wit yo' hat. I can still see it. You always wear that hat? Ain't you burning up?

Grady also informs me my no-name kicks and mismatched clothes are weird. He asks why I'm wearing a Hawaiian shirt and did I buy it because I thought it was cool. He kindly informs me it's not.

A blue pickup truck bumps up the two-lane road.
The man driving waves. Grady waves back.

That's Mr. Mason. He's got chickens. A whole coop. Hey, you talk in yo' sleep? People who stutter can sing without stuttering. Saw it on TV. You should try it.

If Grady pauses, I might tell him my shoes have a name, my beanie *is* hot. That I like my shirt. I haven't kissed a girl except Jacinda in kindergarten, but that don't count. I have no idea if I talk in my sleep, and no, singing won't help. And ignore the part about my face.

Weeds grow high alongside the road. Grady picks a long blade of grass. Silently chews. It's nice. Until he tosses the blade aside.

What you and yo' friends do? Did y'all—

Grady's mouth spouts like a spigot.
My mind stalls on the word *friend*.

This Kid

We hike up roads, some paved, some gravel, to houses
where people sit on porches, fanning themselves.

Grady says Aunt Terri has him deliver to people who can't
get to the market. He explains, *'Cause they're old.*

Every stop, he introduces me. I nod. Give a wave.
And they'll say, *Oh, so you're Vent and Terri's kin. . . .*

Wagon finally empty, we wander past a gas station, A-1 Auto
Shop, Basil's Bar, and Mount Bethel church.

Your uncle was right, says Grady. *You do talk. With yo' eyes
and eyebrows. Hey, you can be a mime.* He brings a cupped
hand to his mouth and slurps. *Get it? Drink. Try it.*
    I shake my head.
Just try.
    I sigh.
This kid is gon' make me dump
a truckload of words on his head.

Where Did They Come From?

This is what I'm thinking when I see two guys working
in Aunt Terri's garden. She reads my mind like it's
her superpower.

Food brings folk together, she says. *Come on.*
I follow her to where they're bent over snipping.
This is Zoomie. He's tall. Wears rain boots.
This is BJ. A big-brimmed hat shades his head.
They, I guess, are about nineteen or twenty.
And this is—she puts a hand on my shoulder—*Isaiah.*

Aunt Terri tells them to show me how to prune okra.
Tells me I'm in good hands. When she's gone,
BJ asks if I know anything about gardening.
I know a li'l something from Mom's plants.
Still, I shake my head *no*.

Zoomie takes his cutters, holds a stalk, pulls a leaf. *This is
a sucker. Get rid of it.* Points to a pod that looks like a
curved finger. *You wanna cut the okra at the stem.* . . .
BJ says, *You eat okra?*
I shake my head *no*.

You will now. He laughs. *These things come in almost every
other day.*
Zoomie says, *They taste all right.*
All right? repeats BJ. *Yeah, if they're fried. But if they're slimy—*
he scrunches his face like okra's in his mouth—*yuck.*
I laugh. They crack up.

I wanna ask why they're here, in the sun, cutting okra,
when they could be doing whatever twenty-year-olds
do down here. But I don't.

I just nod, laugh, cut suckers, snip pods, and think how this,
right here, feels like home when I'm repotting, propagating,
and cutting dead leaves—
except I'm not alone.

The Fellas

Grady looks for me every time he comes for deliveries.
And yeah, I go. But today, it's so hot we drip sweat from
heads to pits. T-shirts stick like skin.

We go to Willie's Beer & Groceries. Narrow aisles crammed
with snacks, motor oil, canned meat, cleaning supplies.
Spy mirrors hang in all four corners, reflecting our every move.

Straight back, refrigerators stock water, soda, and beer.
Grady opens a door. Cool air chills our faces. He snags
a 7UP. I grab a water, remembering how Drew bet me
and Darius to drop Mentos candy into our Cokes and
drink it before it exploded. Pop rocketed all over us.

I pay with four crumpled bills.
Stuff the change in my pocket.

We start out, three boys step in.
                       Hey!   Sup!
              Heads nod. Chins up.
                Dap. Dap. Dap.

Grady's fellas. Hakeem and Antwon who are twins,
both short like him. And Mario who's a little taller.

Grady introduces me as *his* homeboy from up North.
Curious eyes check me out like a specimen.
Hakeem or Antwon points to my tee. *Who's he?*

I ain't said much, don't have much to say. Kinda like not
saying nothing, but I cannot, will not let these kids not know
who *he* is.

My sparse words are measured.
Only one of the greatest guitarists to ever play, I say.
They wait.
Jimi Hendrix.

Jimmy who?   *What's he wearing?*
Don't know his songs.   *He alive?*

Yo, I'm this close to blasting off at the mouth. For real.

Check In

That evening,
Dad calls to see if I'm good.
Asks if I talked to Drew. I haven't.
Yet.

Mom FaceTimes to see my face.
Says I'm healing and still handsome. I agree.
Yes.

Cut Grass

The next day, Uncle Vent waves me off the porch.
Ever cut grass, Son? he asks.
   Yes.
On a riding mower?
   No.

The closest I got to driving was Dad once letting me creep slowly around a half-empty Kroger's lot. I wanted to play it cool, but my hungry hands gripped the steering wheel too tight and couldn't turn. Dad yanked the wheel right before I crashed into the cart return.

Today's your lucky day. Uncle Vent goes over releasing the brake, starting the engine, the five speed levels, and safety precautions. He hands me work glasses, gloves, then instructs me to climb on.

Now, what you might wanna do is start at two. Not quite turtle, not rabbit either.

I do what I remember. He reminds me what I forgot.

My foot lets off the clutch. The mower jerks. I've never ridden a horse, but Dad told me about it. That's how I imagine this to feel. A horse bucking. I laugh. Don't know why. Maybe the thought of Dad on a bucking horse. Or twelve-year-old me grasping the steering wheel too tight.

Uncle Vent laughs too. *You'll get the hang of it.*
He watches a few minutes more, then goes to the porch.

He's right. Soon I'm on rabbit. The motor's rumble transports me to the old West, wrangling horses with Nat Love, chasing bulls with Bill Pickett. I know, I know, I'm too old to be pretending. But I can't help myself.

A silly yeehaw begs to escape.
I look around. No one to see or hear. *Yeehaw.*
A little louder. *Yeehaw!*
Louder. *Yeehaw!!*
Yeehaw! ***Yeehaw!*** ***Yeehaw!***

Grilled Cheese, Yo!

Yardwork on an empty stomach'll have your belly growling like a polecat's.
    Aunt Terri greets me at the back door.
Course, I don't know if polecats growl or not. Never heard one myself.

I sneeze.
She sets down water for my allergy pill.

Aunt Terri makes the cheesiest grilled cheese sandwich.
White bread soaked with butter—and *still* crispy—
got my lips shiny like I been sipping oil. Plus, a slice
of thick bologna and a layer of creamy mustard too.
Bologna and mustard! On. A. Grilled. Cheese, yo!

Boy, don't act like we been starving you down here.
Aunt Terri laughs. *Or is it that good?*
    Yeah, it's that good.
Hmph, must be. Got you saying more than two words.

Aunt Terri sits across from me. Hands me a napkin.

You know, Isaiah, God didn't see fit to let me be somebody's momma. But every now and then She sends me folks to love on like a momma would.

    Aunt Terri fingers her wedding ring.
Your auntie lives to love. And, baby, my love won't let me ignore hurt when it's in front of me.

I wanna tell her I'm not hurt, that I'm okay.
But instead, I tug my beanie down.

Now, I'm not tellin' you you gotta talk. Won't force you to do nothin' you not ready for. But that hurt gots to come out somehow, some way . . . or it'll eat you up, turn you bitter.

    She sits back. Folds her arms.
When you ready, you'll find the way.

Maybe I'm not ready.
Or maybe there's just nothing to say.

What We Do . . .
What We Did?

Grady asks over and over what my friend(s) did up North,
like hanging out would be so different from down South.

My mouth comes out of hibernation to flip
his question back.

Grady wipes sweat from his face with his whole arm. Tells
me they played ball at the rec center, but it closed, nets
taken down. *We still play, though. We oun't need no net.
Got the rim. Hey, you ball?*
> *That's it?* I scoot to the porch's shady spot, dodging
> his question.

Why you think I asked you? Grady stays in the sun. *Ain't you
got something better? Bet you got nothin'.*

Bet.
Sounds like . . .
Drew.
And Darius.

Bet. Got Something.

Four square? Grady shakes his head like bugs on it.
Naw, that's for kindergartners.

I throw up my hands. *Dude, why would I lie?*
Me and my boys ruled that game!

Grady doesn't take my word for it. Still, next day,
we & his fellas meet at a lot they call the Spot.

Nothing but dirt, gravel, abandoned tires, &
to the left, the old netless courts
where a few older boys are hanging out.

I grab the ball. *I'mma take it real easy on y'all,* I say,
sounding more like Drew than me. *Me and my boys merked
this game. Y'all 'bout the same age we were—*

Whassup?   We gon' play or what?
I bounce the ball. *Yeah, ready.*

Grady shifts side to side.
Mario's hands are open.
Antwon's in. Hakeem waits.
I serve.

This game ain't new to them.
Only feels different 'cause of me.
They watch my moves like
I'm the long-leg long-arm fast-moving
LeBron of four square.

Finally, I step out, Hakeem steps in.
They play hard. Sweat harder.
Like Drew, Darius, & I used to.
Exactly like us.

When they're done, they beam at me like
I'm King James himself. Like
I introduced them to the legit best game
in the galaxy. *Y'all got something that tops that?*

Mario says, *I guess, Devil's Slope.*
Devil's Slope? I repeat.
Grady says, *You oun't know what a slope is?*
I say back, *Dude, I know what a slope is.*
Hakeem says, *We ride our bikes down it.*

I figure if *they* can ride this slope, can't be that scary.
Probably nothing but a little dip in the ground.
Definitely not like the mountain.
      The mountain.

Yeah, I say. *Back home we have something like that. But it's a beast. Three stories high . . .* I spin a tale of how *me* & my boys conquered it.

Y'all did? says Grady in awe.
I fold my arms across my chest, stand like the Green Giant.
Yep. We did.
Well, shoot. Grady bounces his ball. *Let's go tomorrow.*

Devil's Slope, pfssh. *Yeah, bet. Tomorrow.*

A Surprise

Back at the house
        a box is on my bed.

Return address
        Frisco Lane.

Inside
        a note.

Just in case.
        Love,
                Mom

My
        camera.

I Try

I click on my camera. There's
Dad taking a picture of Joe Louis's fist.
Mom and her plants.
Drew. Mouth full of donut holes.

I start to call him.

                                            Hang up.

Begin a text.

                                            Delete it.

More and more words spill out

                                            day by day

so how come I can't

                                            find none for him?

He don't wanna hear about me

                                            hanging with
                                      Grady and his crew.

Delivering vegetables grown

                                        in Aunt Terri's garden.

Cutting grass

                                      on a riding lawn mower.

Or would he?

Aye, Drew, you wouldn't believe what happened today. Know how we were shorties on the four square yard . . .

In my mind, I draft a whole day's worth of living that he'll never get to read.

On the Way

Grady leads me through the woods, across a stream,
over dead tree trunks, & up an incline. He on his bike.
Me on Uncle V's, which hasn't been ridden in so long
spiders spun webs through the spokes, making them look
like rims.

Branches slap my arms. Gnats attack my face.
About to turn around, find my way back, when
someone screams.
    What the—
Come on. Grady, all excited, pushes his bike faster.

We enter a clearing where the ground dips.
Older kids, younger kids, groups of girls
hover around with bikes. Each haggling about
whose turn, & nobody's—*nobody's*—reacting to the
    Ahhhhhhhh
growing fainter & fainter.

Grady sweeps his arm left to right. *This is it.*

This Is It?
This is hood Mount Kilimanjaro's twin. *Its twin, yo!*
Can't even see how deep it goes or steep it is because of
the trees. I tug my beanie. *Maaannnn.*

Grady, who's your friend?
I spin around. Face a girl.

Brown skin with patches of light highlights her eyes,
mouth, & fingers. A curly pouf of hair sits on top her head big
like a dandelion. Doc Martens on her feet.

Yo, I'm stuck like T'Challa when he sees Nakia.
Frozen like an antelope in headlights.

Uh, ain't you seen a girl before? she says to me.
Uh-huh, I mumble.
Don't seem like it, she says.

This Isaiah, Grady tells her. To me, he says,
This my bossy sister, Kiana. Hey, you got sisters—
Kiana. Ki-ah-na. Kian—
She looks me over. *Cool band.*

Down I look. Already forgot who's on my shirt. *Five Three Eyes.*
You know *them?*

My mouth curls up, cheesing big.
Muscles tighten around my lips
refusing to fall back into place.

Grady steps between us. *He's here to ride. This ain't nothing,
though, 'cause he rode something way way wayyyy better up
North.*

This kid spills everything I told him. Everything!
I wanna tell him to shut it, but now other kids surround us.
Soared like he had Namor wings. Right, Isaiah?

Oh, that's huge, says Kiana, with a hand on her waist &
her girls at her sides. *Then you can go next, Wing Man.*

I . . . uh, this my uncle's bike. Gotta . . . fix it, I stammer.
She eyes the bike. *Humph. Maybe next time.*

Yeah, sure, I manage. *Next time.*
She climbs her own, rides to the edge, & flies down down
down. Her *See you later!* echoes away away away.

I can't stop cheesing.
Grady groans. *Ew, bro, you smiling at my sister. GROSS!*
Me smiling at Kiana is anything but gross.

Tomorrow

Grady taps my arm. *Wanna come back tomorrow?*

Tomorrow? To this place? To ride down this thing?
I think fast. *Thought you wanted me to show you
what else me and my boys do.*

Better than this? He points behind him.
    Yeah. Most def better.
He gives me an *I don't believe you* scrunch face.

    Dude. One word. Skateboarding.

Skateboarding

Me & Darius used to practice ollies & boneless 180s.
Never did 'em as good as him, but the fellas can't tell.

They take turns balancing & rolling.
They joke, crash, & fall.
We stop for water then at it again until
Hakeem, Antwon, & Mario get bored
of waiting. They take off. Grady stays.

With one foot on the board, Grady
pushes off with the other, wobbling.
He tries again & again.
Gets steadier & steadier.

All the while, I think of ways to ask about Kiana.
Hey, how's your sister?
Hey, how does your sister know Five Three Eyes?
Hey, where does your sister hang out?
But each time I part my lips to ask, I hear a gazillion
questions & a thousand *ewwws* from Grady.

Zoomie and BJ

Swear Aunt Terri grows enough food to feed all of
Salisbury. Told me she would, if she could.
We find Zoomie and BJ out by the old barn turning over soil.
You can help 'em, she says. *If you wanna.*
I wanna.

Zoomie pushes a machine that digs into the ground
and scoops over dirt.
BJ holds a packet of seeds. *We're planting beans.*

I ask why he and Zoomie come here.
Look around, says BJ. *Ain't no grocery stores round here.*
Yeah, says Zoomie. *We live in what you call a food desert.*
And Mrs. Terri, she's like everybody's grocery store.
And Mama, adds BJ. He shakes the seed packet. *We earn
money, plus learn to grow food. And one day we gon'
have our own farm. Ain't that right, Zoom?*

They remind me of Darius dreaming big.
Of Drew making money.
And of me wondering what he's up to.

Fishing

Fishes are as slimy as okra. I ain't lying.
Uncle Vent chuckles when I tell him this.
He says, *But they both taste good.*
I frown, imagining mucusy okra on my tongue. *Not both.*

On his boat we float in the middle of the lake.
Nobody's here but us. And the fish. And the birds.
And the bugs.

Uncle Vent holds a wiggly worm as he describes
the difference between artificial and live lures.
He says words like *crickets* and *crawfish*, *leeches* and
nightcrawlers. Got me itchy all over.

He hands me the worm. When I was little, I played with
them. Even dug them in the garden beds. Now it seems
weird to wrap their little bodies on a hook for bait.

I throw out the line and sit back.
Relax just like my uncle. Take in the silence.
I can get used to this.

Hope

Days later, Antwon & Hakeem skate up with wheels.
Hakeem's got a blue & green board that looks like the ocean.
Antwon's is full of graffiti.

    Now I can tell y'all apart, I joke.

My country days go on like this.
When I'm not at the garden,
I'm skating with Grady & the fellas, &
picturing Kiana, her curly poufy hair,
standing in her Doc Martens, &
secretly hoping she'll ride by.

    She never does.

Leftie

The very next week
I'm showing a trick on my board
when five older dudes wearing durags
roll up like a motorcycle gang
leaning back on souped-up bikes
cool as tricked-out cars.
        I freeze.

A lean one with a wide forehead like Grady's
points his chin my way. *Who dis?*

Grady gives his spiel of me being here for the summer.
Lean one, eyes sharp like metal, nods. *What's poppin'?*
Then, in a *lecture* like way asks if I'm too old to be hanging
around li'l kids.
        I swallow hard. Explain I'm teaching them flips.

Things immediately change
        from scary to shock
when he says, *Oh snap, you da one?*
        I try not to shift. *I'm* the one?

Lean guy introduces himself as Leftie, Grady's brother.—
Whoa, Kiana's brother. He tells how Grady asks
a million questions a day, wears everybody's ears out.
Now all he does is balance on bricks, wanting to do flips.
    Appreciate that, cuz.

The fellas grin & clown Grady, agreeing.
He frowns & brushes them off.

Leftie says, *Li'l bro, getting you a board today.*
Grady's face lights up. *For real?*

Leftie gives me a final once-over, then says, *You straight.*
He nods to the guys. They roll out.
He turns back one last time, warns he's got eyes on me.

Kiana's big brother, who rides with a crew,
with eyes sharp like metal, has eyes on me.

Keep Mowing, Just Keep Mowing

I cut yards for two of Uncle Vent's older neighbors.
Ms. Hurst and Mr. Farmer.

Mosquitoes and gnats rise from the ground,
angry at the disturbance. Still, the wheels keep churning
and the blades keep trimming.

What if there's a record for lawn mowing?

The records . . .

I ride the mower down the road like a car.
Turn up our driveway, park outside the shed.
Dig out my phone. Text Drew.

Me: *Aye*

I study the three letters. A fly buzzes in my face.
I swat at it. Sweat runs down my back.
I wipe at it. I stare at the keyboard.
Why is this so hard?

I type: *Aye guess where I'm at. You wouldn't believe what they got me doing.*

My Hat

Aunt Terri's on the back patio. Soon as I walk up she says,
*Isaiah, why don't you let me wash that hat of yours before it
gets glued to yo' head.*

My hat?
It's been on my head since I got here.
Since before me and Drew fell out.
Since that day in the lot, that day on Rosewood—
since those days.
I'm just not ready.

Still, I ease off my beanie. Hand it over.
She promises to get it back smelling like flowers.
I insist a regular Tide smell is good enough.

I twirl coils in my messy locs, finally understanding
what Superman feels like near kryptonite.

Here, I got this out for you. She hands me a gray cuffed one.
Your uncle's.

Thanks. I pull it on, fast.

Slow down, that hat's not going nowhere. Aunt Terri laughs. And when Aunt Terri laughs, her whole body shakes like it's laughing too.

Makes me wish her house was full of me's to love.

What I Gotta Do

Okay, okay. Yeah, I'm thinking about Kiana.
How she's cute.
Knows Five Three Eyes.
How if I have to go to that slope to see her,
then, yeah, I'll go.

After a bunch of questions about the hat,
I ask Grady to take me.
We meet up with the fellas & yep,
they crack—

Thought that other one was yo' head!
      Where's the snow, cuz?
           A blizzard coming?
I ha-ha 'cause, okay, they're mad funny.

But hoping not funny enough for Kiana to think so.

The Slope

Uncle Vent's brakes still squeak—
Meant to fix them.

Like before, tons of kids wait to ride.
Shrieks pierce the air like we at a haunted house.
I peep around for Kiana.
Spy her with her girls.
Her bike is dark purple & black.
I like purple & black.

Kiana stops talking when she sees me.
I tug on my hat—*Stop,* I tell myself.
She walks over. *Didn't think you were coming back.*
Huh, I grunt.

Mario tells me I got next.
Kiana goes back to her girls. Stops. Turns.
Says, *Good luck.*
Huh, I grunt again. What is wrong with my mouth?
Hey, says Grady. *You okay? Why yo' face look weird?*
A boy is hunched over, eagle ready, soon to swoop.
A wing's beat. He's gone. Nothing left but a cloud of dust.

Hakeem waves me up. I make to go but my legs won't work.
A kid cycles forward. Jumps my spot & rushes off.

You gotta be fast, says Grady. *Y'all not fast up North?*
Antwon shouts, *Go now!*
My knees turn to jelly.
Another kid comes. Skyrockets.

Kiana's all eyes. On me.
I ease to the edge. The tip tip edge.
The slope looks deep. Like DEEP deep.
Kiana crosses her arms.
My hands clench & unclench the handlebars.
    What're you waiting for? Go!
I put my foot on the pedal.
    Hurry up!
I take a deep breath.
    What you gon' do?
Hakeem rolls past & sails.
Antwon comes & flies.
Mario shakes his head. At me. & shoots.
Grady. Soars.

They all go. One by one.
I don't bother to stay & watch.
I back up the bike with its squeaky brakes.
Turn around & ride to Uncle Vent's, alone.

Not Hiding

I hide, I mean, hang out in my room.
Aunt Terri delivers my hat smelling fresh as promised
talking 'bout how she had to bribe it out the washer
talking 'bout how my beanie fell in love with the suds.
You should've heard it, Isaiah. Made me promise
to wash it again next week.

Her jokes almost makes me forget yesterday. *Almost.*

She spots the box on the dresser.
Didn't know you're a photographer too.
Aunt Terri picks up the camera, examines it as if it's
precious stone. She asks what type of pictures I take.

Sky . . . flowers . . . pigeons in rain . . . statues downtown with
my dad . . . my mom trying to skateboard . . . me and my boys
wildin' out . . . all kinds of stuff. Cool, beautiful stuff.

I'm cool. Aunt Terri sets down the camera.
And beautiful. She smiles, winks, and turns to go.

Aunt Terri's smile *is* beautiful.
I mean, for an auntie.

Wait, I call out.
Hold still.

My Phone

I finally get around to checking my phone.
Texts from Mom.
And from Dad.
I text Mom thanking her for the camera.
And Dad, to let him know I'm good.

Not a single one from Drew.
Dad said give him time.
Maybe I didn't give him enough.
I check his socials to see if he's good.
He is.

One Stupid Sentence

Around new people, I don't usually say much, even though thoughts are in my head. When you quiet, you notice a lot of things. Like, people don't like silence. They'll start talking just to fill the space.

Even if what they're saying don't amount to nothing. Even if the talking makes them say something stupid. That's the thing with talking. Can't take back what you say. Or how you say it.

Then you and the person you said something stupid to avoid each other or stop talking at all. Then you feel like an idiot down in Salisbury, North Carolina, sitting in a room staring at your phone.

Face the Music

I hear Grady in the back picking up deliveries.
Don't wanna go to meet him.
Don't wanna answer a million questions about why
I wimped out.

But I gotta face him, the fellas, Kiana too.
Sooner or later. Can't stay in the house forever.

I run out the front door. Catch up with him.
He side-eyes me. Surprisingly, dude's quiet.

We trudge up the road. Him pulling the wagon.
Me with my hands in my pockets. Trucks pass.
Cars too. A wave here. Dog bark there. Finally, I say,

I didn't do that mountain. The one back home.
Crickets.
My friends did. Don't know why I said I did. Naw, I do.
Wanted y'all to think I was big-time. From "up North."

He wrinkles his nose like he smells roadkill.
I was supposed to go back. To do it. But then . . .

I think of the records, how we promised Darius,
& how I screwed everything up.

But then what? says Grady.
Almost forget I was confessing. *Came here.*

Grady switches hands. Wipes his palm on his shirt.
You were scared? It's okay to be scared. You're not too old.
I was scared my first time. Second time too.

Grady says the slope is like a shot, it's scarier thinking about
getting stuck by a needle than actually getting stuck.
A shot can hurt. Got one on my arm. It stung.

It's not until we're near the mobile park that
I have the courage to ask what his sister said.
Grady squints up at me with a *what you think?* look.
That bad? I say.

& he says . . . this kid says,
I can tell you never talked to girls before.

Smooth Dude Move

Dad once told me when things get weird with Mom,
he has a trick. He held up his camera and said,
This always gets your momma smiling again.

I don't have the right words to recite to Kiana
to not have her looking at me like I'm a chump.
So I'm hoping Dad's trick works.

I put on my lucky blue & orange Hawaiian shirt.
Lucky 'cause I look good in it.
Snag my knapsack, go see her,
hoping Leftie doesn't have an eye on me.

She answers the door with *Oh, it's Wing Man.*
Ouch. Okay okay, I can take that. *Hey,* I say.

She holds open the screen door, waiting.
I'm waiting too, for words to fall out my mouth
syrup smooth.

Can I show you something? I finally ask.

She purses her lips. *What?*
I grab my camera out of my bag,
push power &
click through images of
Darius & Drew flipping on boards.
Mom in the greenhouse.
Trappers Alley in downtown Detroit.
The night sky full of stars.

She takes my camera in her hands, does her own
scrolling until she spots a picture of purple toes.
I stiffen.

Are these—she pauses—*yours?*
I nod.
This is it. The part where she says—
I like that color.
What? I blurt. *You don't think it's weird?*
No, she says, looking at me like *I'm* weird for asking.
No? I repeat.
Kiana hands me back my camera. *Clearly you like to stare*
and you're hard of hearing too.

I laugh. But one of those awkward goofy ones.
Kiana crinkles her nose. I clear my throat.

Hey, I say. *Can I take your picture?*
For what? she says back.

For what? For what? Think think think, Isaiah.
My thoughts get smushed together & I vomit, *Because.*

Because—she sits on a step—*is not an answer.*
I drop my eyes, fiddle with the lens, mutter,
'Cause I think you're pretty.

Kiana cocks an ear my way. *Huh? Didn't hear you.*
I sit on a step too & go honest. *'Cause you're pretty.*
She smacks her lips. *Mmmm.*

Bet I know what she's thinking from the way she stretches
out her legs & examines them.

She's got vitiligo. Learned this from Dad's photos.
Vitiligo is when parts of the skin turn pale because the cells
that produce melanin stop working or die.

If I was smooth, I'd tell her vitiligo could cover her entirely
& she'd still be beautiful.

For real, I say.
Kiana punches my arm. *Stop playin'.*
I tell her I'm not. *Here*—I hold up the camera—
lemme show you what I see.

Kiana's lips curl into a half-moon.
Now I get why Dad always takes pictures of Mom.

Flutters

I snap pictures of Kiana
sitting on the steps
gazing directly into my lens,
green-fingernailed hand covering her laugh,
fluffing her poufy hair bigger,
arm outstretched reaching for the camera.

She states, *For the record, I don't need you to tell me I'm beautiful.*
I already know that.

Then she grins wide as Aunt Terri's blossoming peonies.
But I like hearing it . . . from you.

My stomach flutters faster than
my camera's shutter speed.

Grady comes out, skateboard under his pit.
Sees us & groans.

Missed Text

Mom: *Miss you so much! Can't believe you'll be coming home in two weeks. Call me if you need anything. Love you!*

Two weeks?
Two weeks?

I'm going
home
back to where
high school is waiting
Marcus & Randy are lurking
Drew ain't speaking
ghosts of my attack are hovering &
Darius is no longer there.
Naw, I ain't ready
to face none of that.
Not right now &
probably still won't be in
two weeks.

Boating

From the lip of the boat, our lines bob on ripples
enticing fish with their hypnotic dance.
Bubbles explode. But nothing's biting yet.

My line barely wiggles. I sit up. It goes still.
I sit back. Then up. Then back. Can't relax.

My quiet is usually just quiet,
but now it's thinking quiet.
I think of Grady, and me admitting I choked at that stupid slope
and how I always choke.
Of Kiana not needing nobody to tell her she's pretty,
but I can't even admit to liking plants or rock.
Of Darius not being here to walk the halls of Marshall High,
and I wish so badly he was.
Of Drew and our last words,
my stupid last words.
I think about a lot of stuff.
Don't think about a lot of stuff too.

I sigh so loud it drowns out the cicadas.

You okay over there? pipes Uncle Vent.
Yeah, I'm fine.
Not bored, are you?
No. I sip my Sprite and sigh. Again.
Something up? Uncle Vent asks.

Takes me a second before I admit, *Don't think I'm ready to go home, that's all.*
Uncle Vent gives an *is that right?* chuckle.
My mind flashes to him finding me in the backyard with my nunchucks.

Mom said I needed time away like Dad.
Dad needed it because of all he saw.
Said the change did him good. I get it now.

Uncle Vent? I jiggle my line. *My mom tell you everything? Why she wanted me to come?*
Can't say. He holds his beer steady. *Not sure what everything includes.*

Guess that's true. Mom doesn't know everything. *She tell you about my friend Darius?*
Some. He nods. Then adds soft, *I'm very sorry for you.*

Feels like a boa's constricting my throat. I cough to free it. After all this time, why do I still feel bad?

Wanna talk about it? he asks.
An owl hoots. The cicadas buzz.
Naw, I'm good, I say.
But my uncle's unjudging eyes are truth serum,
and I'm *tired*, so tired of holding it in.

I confess how I froze *that* day and things would've been
different if I hadn't.

He rests his beer on top the cooler. His voice serious
when he says, *So you're saying Darius would've heard you
over the shouting?*
I shrug.
And the car driver would've heard you?
I rub my hand over my beanie. *Might've.*
Mmm-hmm. He says, *Seems to me might've ain't a strong
enough answer to torture yourself with guilt.*

I juggle this for a while. I do blame someone else too.
I tell my uncle about the man and how I asked Dad why
dude was mad. Tell him how Dad said something about
ignorance and complicated.

Mmm-hmm. He grunts. *Isaiah, all I can say is, man is man.
We act on our nature. We make choices. Good, and bad.
Most of us try to be more good than bad. Others, well,
they reason their bad is good. Justified. Don't care how it
hurts others. But we all make choices.*

That's supposed to help me when I go back home?

Isaiah. Uncle Vent continues. *I'm gon' tell you like my daddy told me and your momma. Your shoulders might get heavy, head even drop low, but walk tall like you belong in this world, 'cause you do. Hold yo' head high, 'cause it's your birthright. You got a right to joy and peace and whatever else you want. Understand?*

I inhale his words. Words from my grandfather.
My rights. Never heard it put that way before.

And if that's the case . . . No, not *if*.
That's the case.

Me & Kiana

Today, me & Kiana
walk side by side
her carrying a bag of
microwaved popcorn as
Meet Me @ the Altar
bops from her phone
like a soundtrack.

She shares with me her
secret thinking place
which is really a small opening
hidden behind a canopy of trees
& not so secret.

We sit on a huge rock
that's been spray-painted
over & over
words hardly readable.

I take off my knapsack. *Supe place.*
A yell. Way off. *Devil's Slope near here?*
Yep. She points. *Down that way. You gon' do it?*

I shrug. *Maybe.*
Maybe?
I hear the *you scared?* hidden in her voice.

We dig our hands into the bag
grabbing small fingerfuls
stuffing salty popcorn into our mouths
as mosquitoes nick our blood.

She points to a huge tree with bark
that looks like an elephant's leg &
branches that hang like elephant trunks.

That's the revenge tree, she says. *Lore has it
this guy brought a girl here on Valentine's Day
to dump her. Now every Valentine's, she comes back
for blood. If you're a guy, don't be caught here
on February fourteenth.*
Is that true? I ask.
Only if you believe. She grins, slyly.

We reach the bag's bottom
our fingers touch
lingering until it's   awkward.

She asks why I'm so quiet.
I shrug. *I dunno.*
But I do know I like it here.   With her.

Kiana wipes her hands on her shorts.
Got something.
From her sling bag she pulls out
a bottle of black polish.
For you.

She takes my hand.
I jerk it back.
I'm snatched right into
our living room with my
purple-painted toes.

I Got Rights

I flash back to what my uncle said
about my right to joy
& whatever else I want.
But still, I'm not so sure. . . .

Kiana asks if I'm okay.
I tell her *yeah* & ask
if she knows any boys
who wear polish.
She says, *I know you.*

My heart jumps when
I give Kiana my hand.
She starts at my pinkie,
paints one by one,
ending with my thumb.

You like? she says, when done.
Yeah. Why, though?
She caps the bottle. *Why not?*

Who Got Pull?

Gnats swarm in chaotic clouds.
No-see-ums see us.
She swats them back. We beg for peace.
Kiana's left knee leans into my right.
Sweat collects but I don't move
not a single inch because this is the first time
I've sat this long with a girl.

In this stillness, Rosewood lingers.
Wish I had black fingertips then.
Maybe I would've screamed like Jimi's guitar.

In this ease, I tell Kiana my best friend died.
She asks how.
I say, *Car. Accident.*
She says how sorry she is.
She rests her hand on my knee. Asks if I'm okay.

I'm about to say yes, but truth, I'm mad.
Mad about Darius. Mad at myself. Mad at Drew.
Mad about what happened to me.
But that's too much to say. Right now.

Right now, I just wanna feel the small drop of sweat
rolling from my knee where it meets Kiana's.

I ask a question I've been curious about since day one.
How you know Five Three Eyes? I tell her how kids at
school wear retro tees & don't know the band or artist,
can't even name a song.

She laughs & tells me it was on a playlist Spotify created.
I tell her I never met someone who knows them. *Who else
you listen to?*
  Oxymorrons.
Me too.
  The New Respects.
Me too!

Soon we're listing bands & creating playlists.
Soon I'm telling her how I hid rock like a F minus
all because I was teased by two jerks.
Soon I'm telling her Drew discovered the posters
hidden in my closet, how I freaked, & how he ain't react
like I thought. Actually, I don't know what he thought
'cause he don't talk about nothing.
  Kiana is a sponge & soaks up my words.

Her neck rolls like a coaster when she tells me how she's
been called Oreo 'cause of her skin, taste in music, & clothes.
But nobody's got enough pull to take away her vitiligo, so
why should she care what anybody has to say.

I tap my nails, gentle, make sure they're dry.
Another faint yell.
You think I'm scared to do it, don't you?

Kiana purses her lips.
She's even cuter when she purses her lips.
To be honest, I don't care if you do or don't.
I mean, it's your life, ain't it?

She doesn't care?
She won't think I'm weak . . . or soft . . . or nothing?

Kiana picks at the rock like she's moved on.
She probably has.

But not me. I'm still stuck on what she said,
which is mixing with Uncle V.'s talk about my rights.

I mean, they have a point.
It is my life. Mine.

Nails So Black

Nails so black I'm wicked.
Nails so black I'm Egyptian high-class.
Nails so black looks like onyx from the earth.
Nails so black my fingertips shout they're proud.

    I am
    a fist-pump-in-the-air me.
    A roar-like-a-tiger me.
    A *why I been hiding this side of me?* me.

And   still
    still
I'm kinda nervous what people'll say
when they see this black polish side
    of me.

Seen

Every day Aunt Terri's plucking & pulling & planting.
Like Mom.

She twists a spigot & water shoots up from hoses in the ground & gently sprays the tomatoes, cabbages, & cucumbers. She hands me gloves. I reach out. She spies my fingers.

Hmph, well, you are full of surprises, aren't you?
What made you polish your nails?

I tell her Kiana did. Aunt Terri's lip smack says she wants the full story. So I go back to my toes.

Told you what's in you gon' come out. She winks. *I think the world'll be a better place if we just learn to shut our mouths and let people be. If you like your nails polished, then I love it.*

She slides her hand in a glove & adds, *Now it won't bother me or your uncle none. But of course, you've got to answer to your parents.*

Yeah, I say. *I know.*

Thinking of a Master Plan

The next morning, I'm up early.
Roosters don't even get up this early.
But Aunt Terri does.
She blows into a mug.
Working in the garden today?
      Not today. Going biking before Grady comes.
She tells me to be back for breakfast.

I oil the bike's chain, check the brakes & gears—
      Everybody wants me to do the slope to prove I can.
                                               For them.

I ride up the road, through the woods—
                                But I wanna do it.
                                For me.

To the path that leads to—

Devil's Slope

It's like a huge asteroid fell from the sky
blasted a hole in the earth.

I cup my hands over my mouth. *Hello!*
Hello hello hello soars through the trees,
across to the other side.

I hike down the trail, noting the curves & bumps.
The tree stumps & root lumps. Where it veers off to the
right like a mystery. Come to a fork, eye left, right, exploring
which route's best. At the very bottom, there's a curve
that swoops up like a devil's horn. Whoa.

I get back to the top. Hop the bike.
Ride down. Slow slow.
Force my arms to loosen. Easy easy.
Let go of my tense grip. Chill chill.
Hit a hump then a bump. *Dang!*
Fall & bust my butt. *Dag!*
Start again. & again.

The next morning, I climb back up.
There, waiting with the biggest, cheesiest grin, is
Grady.

He jumps up & down, flapping his arms like a hawk.
I knew it! I knew it!
Spooked birds squawk from nests.
Startled squirrels scatter up trees.
& Grady's steadily jumping.
Knew you were up to something!

Detective Grady

I came for deliveries. Miz Terri said you already gone. I said, Where? She said, I oun't know. So you been coming here? Why? Ain't nobody here. You still scared? I know some scared—

Grady. When he stops talking, I tell him I had to learn on my own when to swivel the handlebar left, right, sharp, fast. To lean forward without falling. To be loose like water.
    Be like water.

Aye, ever heard of Bruce Lee? I ask.
He nods.
I tell him a short story about Darius & Bruce Lee.
He scratches his head. *Be like water?*
I move my hand like a snake. *Yeah, water flows like this. Easy. I told your sister—*

My sis—Grady clocks my fingers.—*You know you got paint on yo' nails? My sister do that to you?*

Grady informs me I'm a boy & he ain't ever seen a boy wear polish. Not around here. Asks if that's how boys do up

North. Says he ain't gon' wear polish even if it is for a cute girl & his sister ain't even cute.

When he stops for a breath, I don't tell him I disagree about his sister, but do tell him my plan.

I hold out my fist. *You got me?*
He eyes it. Probably thinking how he had my back a week ago & I let him down. Grady must forgive me because he raises his to meet mine.
All right. My dude.

Flow

Everybody's at the slope. Grady & the fellas. Kiana &
her girls. Even Leftie & his crew. Taking bets—on *me*.

Riders go down squealing.
Some play it cool, then scream halfway out.

Grady taps my shoulder. *You next.*
I rode up & down this crater plenty.
Still, my arms shake as I hand Grady my knapsack.

Right foot on the pedal. *Okay, I got this.*
In three,
        two,
                one!—
                      I fly like an arrow!

                                  Be like water.
Branches whip my face. Bushes scratch my legs.
                                  Be like water.
I hit bumps, dips, tree roots too. I stand up, crouch low.
                                  Be like water.
I flow left, right, skid, swerve. Down, down, down.

I freakin' flow like water! *Like water, yo!*
Wait, where that hump come from?!
Bam!—
I sail headfirst into a bush.
Leaves stick to me like dew.
Footsteps pad. Close, closer.
I roly-poly out. Kiana stands over me.
You okay? The bump got you, didn't it?
I bust out laughing. *That was freakin' amazing!*

Well, duh, she says, laughing too.
Grady bounces, holding up my knapsack.
Can I take a picture for proof! Can I?
I lie right there smiling at the sky.
Fiiinnne.

We climb back up. Kids soar past like blurs.
Some slam down around us. Crash into trees.
We get to the top. My heart still pounds!

Grady shouts, *You weren't scared this time? You know you scream like a girl? You should go again.*

Kids clap my back. Leftie nods approval.
Hakeem, Mario, & Antwon give daps.
My chest pounds like a marching band.
& I cannot, will not, stop grinning.

Kiana grabs my hand.
Ew, not that again, says Grady.
Grady, she says in her big sister voice.
We'll see you later.

What? We just got started.
She squints.
He retreats &
gives Kiana the evil eye for stealing me.

This kid.

Unbelievable

Me: *Can't believe it. . . . That's no baby slope. . . .*
Kiana: *How did you not see that bump?*
Me: *I don't know. Thing sent me flying.*
Kiana: *Were you scared? Tell the truth?*
Me: *Yeah, a li'l bit. . . .*

Kiana laughs while my mouth blabs. Can't help it.
Fifteen minutes later we're at the rock & I'm still yapping.
I was swerving . . . then skidding . . . then soaring . . .

Kiana climbs up. I park the bike, climb up too.
She unties her boots. Tosses them on the ground.

Know what I wish? Wish my boys could've seen me.
Dang. *My boys.*

She says, *You got a picture.*
I check my camera. *Yo, Grady cut off my head!*
We laugh. Till we don't.
Except for the scatter of birds in bushes, it's quiet.
Boating-on-the-lake quiet. Thinking quiet.

I'm going home soon. I tell Kiana I got a week left.
Should've told you sooner.

Been having such a good time,
I haven't worked through things back home.
Darius. Drew. The Yelling Man.
It's all waiting for me.

Kiana takes my hand. *You picking off the polish.*
Half is gone from my thumb.
She doesn't ask what's on my mind.
But the question thrums on her fingertips.

Ever been scared? I ask.
Kiana tells me lots of times. Tells me about a girl, Trish.
With a gang of girls, Trish tried to jump her, after school.
Could've peed myself I was so scared. But I ain't run.
She points to a scar on her wrist. *You?*

Yeah. I tell her about the garage jumping,
backflipping, & mountain riding.

My knee bounces.
She rests her hand on it.

I tell her about wheelie popping day.
The man. The car. Drew keeping it in.
Me wanting it out.

She squeezes my knee.
Don't know why I'm blabbing this now.
Maybe because I *am* kinda nervous to go back home.

I explain how I rode down Rosewood for Darius.
How the man came yelling. How I started to bike away.
But turned back. Faced him. Yelled. Then sped away 'cause yeah, I was scared. Mad scared.

You didn't keep riding away. That counts. She traces her scar.
I touch my face where my bruise had been. *But does it?*

I Brought It on Myself

If I stayed off Rosewood, kept my mouth shut,
then what happened wouldn't've happened.

Kiana asks what I mean. *You can ride down that street.*
He ain't have the right to stop you.

Yeah, but . . .
I tell how I went straight to the lot to meet Drew.
Then outta nowhere the two men came charging.

How they tackled me.
How my knees hit the ground.
Thought my caps broke.

I was like, What I do?
But they ain't answer.

I tell how they wrestled me.
How I tried to fight back.
I did try.

Again, I was like, What I do?

One smushed my head in the gravel.
Rocks cut into my face.
His nose at my nose. Breath sour.
I seen you casing my street.
You dealing drugs? Breaking into houses?

Now I'm talking loud. Mad loud.
But I can't stop.
Me? Drugs? Breaking into houses?
Now I'm breathing heavy. A *mad* heavy.
Mad they followed me! Mad they accused me!

Kiana, I stay outta trouble.
They knocked Pods out my ears—
grinded knees in my back.
Shoved my head down, hard. Hard!—

And then, then I saw Darius
twitching on the ground.
Kiana . . .

I ain't never been that scared in my life.
Still—
I wrestled like I'm Lee, Jabbar, and Kelly.
But those men who grabbed me were big. Strong.
And I gave up.
I gave up. . . .

They wanted to know my name.
Why I was there.

I was terrified.
Too terrified to speak.

All I could think
to say
was . . .

i'm just a kid

just turned fourteen
don't hurt me
oww, your knee
in my back
isaiah
that's
my name
that's my bike
over there
i didn't do nothing
oww, please
that hurts
my friend got hit
on your street
he died
on the ground
we were breaking
records owww let me up
please
am i
gonna
die—

Fine

My hands earthquake shake.
Don't realize it until Kiana covers them.

I'm fine, I mumble.
She looks right through my lie. Says,
You don't have to say you're fine if you're not.

Roar

After a while
Kiana hops up. *Come on.*
I climb up.

She shouts—*Ahhhhhhhhhh!*—
then looks to me & says,
Sometimes you gotta get it out.

She's Mom's purple polish.
Magic.

I open my mouth & let it rip.

Rewind Time

I take my camera everywhere I go.
Rewind time like old photos.

I take pictures of neighbors on their porches
People walking from Willie's Beer & Groceries
Leftie & his boys cruising like a motorcycle gang
Grady & the fellas skateboarding
Kids daring Devil's Slope
The lawn after I mow it
Zoomie & BJ pruning okra
Folks waving thanks for Aunt Terri's vegetables
Grady pulling the wagon
Vendors selling goods at the farmers market
Uncle Vent & his boat
Aunt Terri in her garden

But mostly
of Kiana.

Rewind Kiana

We go to the rock one last time.
From a paper bag, Kiana pulls out purple spray paint.
Gotta leave a mark. Say you were here.

I shake the can, wondering what to write.
I push the button. A hiss sprays out as I scrawl
ISAIA-AHH-AHH-AHH!

She rests a finger on her chin, interpreting.
I say, *It's a spin on the roar from "Immigrant Song."*
Ahh. She nods. *Which reminds me.* She gets her phone,
sends me a link. *A playlist I made for you.*

I ping her back. Grinning. *Yo, I made one for you too.*
The air gets mad mushy until
Kiana whips up her cell for a selfie.
We frown, smile, & stick out tongues.

One last one, she says. *Ready?*

We lean our heads together—*click!*
Kiana turns to me—*click!*

Kisses my cheek—*click!*
Wait, kiss my cheek!—*click!*
I face her—*click!*
She leans in—*click!*
Kisses my lips—*click!*

Grady is so wrong.
His sister ain't nearly gross.

Rewind Grady

Me & Grady deliver vegetables one last time together.
The older men & ladies are now like grandparents,
offering us hard candy & chips. Laughing as Grady spits
sentences that don't end.

Wagon on empty. Grady's questions on full.
*My sister your girl now? She ain't that pretty. She okay
for a sister. Hey, you gon' wear that polish home?*

If I could, I'd tell him I ain't sure if his sister is my girl.
Haven't asked her. Tell him she's pretty & smart too.
& yeah, I'mma wear the polish home.

We take the wagon around back.
Grady parks it by Aunt Terri's shed.
We practicing flips today?

Sure, I say. *But first lemme show you the best thing EVAH.* . . .
Ever cut grass?

I show Grady the gears, the brake, & give him safety
precautions. Convince him to cut Mr. Farmer's &

Ms. Hurst's grasses. Tell him about the Black cowboys &
cowgirls who Dad took pictures of so he can imagine himself
out West too.

His greedy hands grip the steering wheel.
You gon' let me do the whole yard?
I shake my head. *Naw, two rows, then it's all me.*

For one last time, I mow Uncle Vent's lawn. Don't care
about the heat or sweat. Not the mosquitoes hunting
like vampires or the grass blades shooting like shuriken
stars. Naw, I take my time.

Rewind Uncle Vent & Aunt Terri

It's time.
Uncle Vent shakes me awake.

It's not even five a.m.
I heave myself out of bed.

Aunt Terri's already on the porch, waiting for the sun.
The smell of brewed coffee floats in the air.

She gives me the up and down. *Look at you. From the way
you walk, even the way you stand, almost don't recognize
the boy who waltzed into my kitchen six weeks ago.*

She faces the horizon.
It's been good having you here, Isaiah.

I remember what she said when I first got here.
What's inside me gots to come out.

She was right.
Thanks, Aunt Terri.

We go out on the boat.
Me and my uncle.

The sun's not woke yet. My eyes droop.
Fish bite. I wake up quick.

Looka here. Uncle Vent points to my line. *Reel it in.*
I pull up on the pole, turn the knob thing, and whoa—
a small fish dangles and wriggles like it's fighting for its life.

You know . . . He helps me gently ease the hook from the
fish's lip. *You're gonna have to tell your mom and dad
something.*

Mom's been worried about me since I was born.
But especially since *that* day. *I know.*

The sun breaks over the tips of the trees.
Soft rays sneak through the leaves.
The fish flips about in my hands.
Still fighting. I hold it firm. Ready to drop it in the bucket.

It still wriggles. Still fights.
I stop.

I lean over the edge of the boat.
And let the fish go.

Reverse Home

We load the trunk. Aunt Terri's swearing how I shot up
at least three inches since getting here.

I'm wrapped in her goodbye cocoon.
Before she lets go, I say, *Aunt Terri,*
think you can fix me a grilled cheese? For the road?

Boy—she throws her head back laughing—*anybody tell you*
you can eat?

She makes me two.

Home

Uncle Vent pulls into the drive. Our house looks
brand-new and familiar at the same time.

Mom planted flowers. Like, hundreds. Like
she went to a garden store and couldn't decide which
ones to buy, so she bought 'em all.

We pile inside, wiped from the eleven-hour ride.
We drop my bags. Good thing, because either Mom's gotten
stronger, or me weaker. Her tackle almost takes me down.

My face in her hands gets clobbered with kisses.
She pulls away, studies me, and cries,
A baby mustache. You've gotten taller. Polish too.

Uh-oh.

Then, I hear, *Let the boy breathe.*
And it ain't Uncle Vent.
Dad?
Surprise! He grabs me, pulls me in. *Missed you.*

I don't keep my missing inside. *Missed you too.*
Just don't kiss me like Mom.

Mom rubs my head—*without* my beanie—and says,
He don't have to kiss you like me because he's taking you
for a haircut. ASAP.

Should've known that was coming.

Change Is Cool

Mom wants to know everything—*everything*—
I did down South. I tell her about Grady and the deliveries,
the fellas and their skating, the gardening, the mowing,
the boating. And Kiana and her fingernail painting too.

Dad nods. *Oh, Kiana.*
Mom smiles. *Kiana? Ooh.*
Uncle Vent *mmmm-hmmms.*

I hold up my hand and ask what I've been anxious to ask,
Are you okay with this?
A pause. A pause so brief and so loud,
I can't help but hear what they don't say.

Still, it's their *yes* I catch.

What Needs to Be Said

I'm not sure if I'm ready to face
all the stuff that's happened, but facts—
it felt better talking about it with Kiana
and Uncle Vent.

My uncle's right too, I do have to tell
Mom and Dad about *that* day.
Just wish I could bring his boat and the lake
into our living room.

I take them back in time like a historian
laying out the events since Darius's death—
my guilt, classmates acting funny, Drew shutting down,
the wheelie, Rosewood, and finally,
the lot—

They're quiet, faces contorting, sorting
through my words like
sifting through sand for a shell.

Suddenly, Mom gets up, paces back and forth
from one end of the couch to the other.
She goes from wanting to cradle me like a toddler—
Knew something was wrong. Baby, are you okay?—
to Mama Bear ready to roar, rumble, and report—
I'm calling the police . . . need to investigate—

Dad repeats low,
I could've lost you. I could've lost you? I could've lost you—
gaining momentum until he says it one last time—

I COULD'VE LOST YOU

He
      grabs me   holds me
                      close
buries my head   in his chest   his
heart beats   hard and loud   like   a
    battle cry
his arms around me   strong   like   a
fortress   I don't push away
     we stay   like this   locked in place
              both of us
     breathing   heaving   sighing
for   seconds   minutes   months
                 until
the tight   in my neck   shoulders   throat
            until
everything   everything
seeps from me slow   like water   and
    drips to the   floor
       pools around   our feet   and evaporates
              then
finally   he lets   go.

When Dad releases me, he wipes his eyes.
Mom said Dad doesn't cry, not even when he entered that church after the mass shooting. Said he almost did but didn't.
    Today, Dad cries.

When Dad releases me, I wipe my eyes.
Dad once told Mom I needed to be toughened up.
I was seven. Haven't cried since, even though
I might've wanted to.
    Today, I bawl.

Knock-Knock

The sandman can dump thousands of tiny grains
on top of my head, and I'll still be awake.

Thoughts play knock-knock at my brain's door.
Knock-knock?
    Who's there?
Didn't ya?
    Didn't ya who?
Didn't ya foul some stuff up?
    Shut up.

Drew's words clear in my mind: *My dad's in jail.*
My words, just as clear. *What he do?*

I slam my fists into the bed.
Stupid. Stupid. Stupid.
He didn't have to do nothing; I get that.
The words just came out. Came out wrong.
I had questions and I care and I—
messed up. I messed up.

Peace

It takes five minutes to force myself to Drew's building.
Soon as I hit the breezeway under the stairs, I about jump—
Yo! You scared me.

Drew looks up from his bike. Eyes grow big like golf balls,
then deflate fast. *Shouldn't scare so easily.* He stands.
Whassup, Country Boy. So, you back, he says like
we never beefed.

I wobble. Caught off guard. *Yeah. Got back yesterday.*
He smirks. *Yo, your hair.*
Sides shaved close with a box of locs on top.
Yeah, hella different. I rub over my coils.

He notices my nails.
His frown tells me this is something else
he can't rock with.
That's it, I think. *We're done.*

Then he kicks the stand of his bike and walks.
I follow him into the parking lot.

Drew straddles his bike. *Yo, you bumpin' to
that country music now?*

I drop my board, hop on top, and rock. *I listen to it all.
You know me*—I catch myself. He don't know me.
He looks around like he's got someplace to go. *So, what's up?*

I finger one of the scratches from Devil's Slope.
Flick off the scab. It disappears in the wind.
I texted you.
Yeah, my bad. Been—
Busy, I say. *Figured.*

Already we've run out of things to say,
even though we got tons. And now this
mad awkward silence is doing all the talking.

Drew eyes the gathering clouds, then looks to his
apartment like he's about to bounce.
My thumbs hooked tight under my knapsack straps.
I'm hoping he doesn't.

I had half the summer to think about what to say.
Never could figure it out. *Dude*, I start, *didn't know you had
all that going on.*
He shifts.
Guess you had stuff and I had stuff.
With a stone face Drew says, *You rode over here
to say that?*

With a stone face I say back, *Nah. I came because—*
All night I thought how his distance and secrets became
reminders of how I no longer fit in his world unless *he*
needed my quiet. Everything on his terms.
So why did I come?

*I came to apologize. . . . Tried to say something sooner but
couldn't put the right words together.*
Noticed, says Drew.

Dude, I know you noticed; I get it. I rock on my board. *But
dang, bro, you shut me out. And I ain't tryin' to make this
about me, but things got grimy—*
Grimy for you? Yeah, okay. He kicks the pedal. Scans the lot.

His face the same as the last time I saw him.
Straight up looked like he hated me.
Get the hell on.

I don't go nowhere.

Real Talk

All this time he had me believing his dad was in the army. And I don't know why. So, I ask Drew how come he never told me the real deal about his father.

He kicks the pedal again. *'Cause*—his eyes shine like a tiger's—*of that look on your face that I thought maybe, hoped maybe, you wouldn't have. But when I did tell you, you did, bro. You had disgust. Pity. I oun't need that. Don't need no stupid questions faked up with concern like "How you feel?" either.*

Yeah, I would've asked that, but it wouldn't've been fake. Might've been stupid. I mean, how would anybody feel? How would *I* feel? And my face, the stupid look on my face, was the thing. It was *the* thing?

I didn't mean to have that look. I really didn't, yo. I was just . . . I don't know, I was thinking that we're boys and—

Drew snorts. A *that was kinda funny* snort.
       What? I say.
Dude, sometimes you clueless with yo' big house, expensive

*skateboards, closet full of clothes. Bro, you got tons of kicks
you don't even wear!*

    *I know, but it doesn't mean nothing. Dude, it's just
stuff—*

Just stuff? Drew claps, saying, *Bro, you making my point.
I could take five pairs of yo' sneakers. You wouldn't even know.*
    I picture my closet. He's right. A ton's in there.

*You even know I wash my laces every night in the sink? Brush
the soles with a toothbrush to keep my joints fresh?*
    I . . . didn't.

He keeps going. *Bro, we cram into an apartment.
Me and Marvin share a room. He can't get too cold,
so it's a furnace in there. He gets tired. Always hurting.*

A drop of wet hits my hand. I ignore it. Can only think how
I haven't thought, *should've* thought, about Drew's day-
to-day with his brother. Dang, all this time, I *have* been
all me me me. How could I not see that?

Dude. He bounces his front tire, hard. *I ain't got enough of
anything. So I hold tight to what I do got. And my dad's
part of that.*

Drops get heavier. We move into the breezeway.
His face is fierce. *When I go MIA, it's 'cause we drive four
hours to see him—for only an hour—drive four hours*

back. *Sometimes we still don't get to see him.* Drew's chest heaves. *Why I wanna tell you that?*

He drops his bike to the ground. *And when you asked—you asked—*he claps each word like thunder—*What. He. Did —dude, what he did?*

His claps are gut punches. I want so bad, so so bad, to take those words back. *Drew, I didn't mean how it sounded. Swear I didn't. It came out wrong.* And I know *these* words don't make it right. Know they're not enough.

Drew's voice cracks like rain splitting pavement. *Wanna know so bad why my dad's locked up?*—It don't matter now. Not to me. Not like that. But he doesn't give me time to answer.—*Lapse of car insurance. No car insurance!*

He squeezes his eyes shut.
Rain runs down his cheeks.
He doesn't wipe.
He crosses his arms defiantly.

We was taking Marvin to the doctor. We got stopped. Po-po talkin' 'bout we rolled through a stop sign. Told him to get out the car. My dad asked, "Why?"—Drew gets louder.—*They were like "You gon' be a problem?" A problem? For asking a question, yo! My dad said, "I got my sons. Gotta get to the doctor."*

Rain pelts the pavement loud like drums.
Drew shouts over the beating. *They yanked him out—*

My mind flashes to that day with the Yelling Man. How they wrestled me down. Grinding gravel in my face.

Threw him to the ground! Said he was resisting!
He wasn't! Ask Marvin! Years of his life for a lapse of car insurance!

Drew punches at the sky. Shadowboxes with ghosts of *wish I could. Wish I could've said something . . . wish I could've stopped 'em . . . wish I could've helped . . .*

His world was crashing down all around him.
Every day. And I didn't know.
We're supposed to have each other's back.
That's what *we* three said. We gave our word. *Our word!*

I step closer, swing my fists at the sky too.
We both fight battles. Knock 'em out. Side by side.
We punch and yell. Yell and punch. Until we don't.

Breathe

We sit at Drew's kitchen table. Silent. Exhausted.
His mom's sausage & eggs bring him back to himself.
Laughing & joking about how silly I look in his clothes.
At least they dry, I joke back.

We eye each other.
Only now noticing the changes.

You got a little swole, I say.

                            Drew flexes. *You got dark.*

You got a little taller too.

                               Man, taller than you.
                               Yo, see your li'l stache.

Little? I rub the fuzz like it's full grown.
You too.

                              Yeah, got a li'l something.
                              You painting your nails now?

Yeah. Kiana did this.

                            Drew raises a brow. *Kiana?*

You still talking to Vanessa?

                                   Yeah, we good.

I tell him about Grady, his fellas, &
teaching them our tricks.
He tells me he's going out for football.
You should see me. Yo' boy got skills.

Yo, I almost forgot. I get my soaked knapsack.
Pull out a baggie. Hand it to him.

He holds it away from himself. *What's this?*
The best grilled cheese sandwich you'll ever eat in your life.

Still, there's more
unsaid
undone
unsomething
that blocks us from picking up
where we left off before all the before.

Aight, Got One . . .

I dig at my eggs & say, *Aight, got one.*
I start the game of stupid questions for random answers.

Dance or stunt challenge?
Drew smirks. *Man, easy. You know I'm dope with both.*
His non-answer breaks the rules. I aim my fist—
Wait. Stunts. What's the one food you could eat every single day for life?
Not burgers, I joke, reminding us of our Bubba's Burgers disaster.
My aunt's grilled cheese.

Okay, here's another. . . .
Wanna try again . . .
for Darius?

Drew goes mum.

The mountain, I say.
We promised.

The Beast

Me & Drew stand again in front of the
hugest dirt mound around.

Darius was right, I say, looking up. *It's about three stories.*
You ain't gon' flake, are you? says Drew.
Nope.

I don't tell him about Devil's Slope.
Don't talk trash either.

I push my bike forward. *Watch the student become the master.*
Bet? he says.
Bet, I say.

I block out how I froze.
How I tripped, fell, & slid down like gravy.

I climb to the top without stopping.
The bottom looks miles away.
I hear Darius's voice: *Be like water.*

I count down from five to one & shove off!
I ride the beast's back like a bronco buster.
Zip & swerve & glide & ride & dag!—
hit a bump &—
I flyyyyyy!

& yo, it was *bananas*!

Frozen Moments

On my dresser is my camera
I switch it on and am immediately reminded
of what I already miss:

Aunt Terri's grilled cheese, shrimp and grits
butter beans and corn bread
Uncle Vent and his boat and the lake and the quiet
Kiana on the rock, painting my nails, me snapping
shots of her
Grady's questions that don't end
Mowing the lawn
And yeah, even Devil's Slope.

Marshall High

I'm in my closet figuring what to wear
to not stand out, look different, or weird
when my phone dings.

Kiana: *Happy first day of school. Welcome to the jungle.*
Jungle. Funny. Oh snap—
"Welcome to the Jungle." Guns N' Roses.
I type back with a smile on my face.
Same to you.—& hit her with another title.—*Rocket Queen.*

I ease my Guns N' Roses 1989 concert tee off the hanger,
slip on a pair of ripped jeans with lots of zippers, &
top off my 'fit with my orange-cream-&-blue Hawaiian shirt.
Then I grab five envelopes off my desk & stuff them in my
bag for Drew.

Mom grabs her keys. *I'll take you.*
Mom—
It's the first day, Isaiah, she says.
Her *pretty please* look gets to me. *Fine,* I say.

We pull up in the car line. I grab the door handle &
glimpse my painted nails. Immediately I hear Grady's voice.
You know you got paint on yo' nails?   That kid.

If Grady was here, I'd explain only my thumb, pointer, &
pinkie is polished—The rock sign.—& not my whole hand.
Not yet. I'm not trying to get stuffed in no locker. Baby steps.

Before I get out, Mom rubs my locs, free of my beanie.
My baby, she says.
I don't gripe how I'm not a baby, because yeah, I'm hers.
Whatever.

Suddenly, I'm in the throes of hundreds of kids walking tall,
laughing loud, hovering about, gabbing & joking.
Suddenly, I don't know how to move, or how to hold
my book bag. Straps over both shoulders? One strap
strung over one shoulder? Hanging loosely from my hand?
I'm frozen for seconds, for minutes in front of this
humongous beast of a school.
The beast.

Even though me & Drew conquered that mountain,
I get the feeling that high school ain't a slope.
My brains tells me, *Be tough, Isaiah.*
Asks, *What happened to the what-they-say-don't-matter Isaiah?*
And the you-got-a-right-to-whatever Isaiah?

I can't say nothing back because my mind is scattered,
my tongue is limp, & my palms won't stop sweating because
here I am, the first year since sixth grade, with no Darius &
no—

Yo, don't tell me you about to choke. Drew.
He laughs. I breathe.
Naw, I lie & spy his shirt. Wu-Tang.
He sees me gawking. *Yo, don't even start. I know all the lyrics
to every one of their songs.*
I tell him he can borrow one of my tees anytime.
He frowns. *Yeah. Bet.*
                                                              Bet.

Oh, got something. I get the envelopes out of my bag.
Drew raises a brow. *Guinness?* He rips into one.
Whoa, don't get too excited. I pat his shoulder. *Only
certificates, not money.*

Before I forget. Drew reaches into his bag & shoves
something at *me.*
I unravel a ball of fabric. & cheese harder than a mouse
with a slice of cheddar. *Yo, a Prince tee? Whaa, you
listening to—*

Naw, he ain't rock. So don't start tripping. Drew stuffs his
hands into his pockets. *I know you're a purist and this
ain't one of your "authentic" ones, but—*
Bruh, I say, cutting him off. *I ain't got a Prince. Thanks.*

Marcus & Randy call to Drew. He raises his chin to them.
To me, he says, *Yo, I gotta go.*
Five seconds of silence, then Drew lifts his hand.
Aye, be like water.

I glance around, a part of me still expecting—
no, wanting—to see Darius.
I lift my hand too.
We front hand slap our clap & end with a palm clasp.
& I say, will only ever say,
Always.

Acknowledgments

In 2019, my first novel, *Genesis Begins Again*, made its debut. And my word, it was and still is well received. For that, I am grateful.

Then came the fear. *How can I write such another book? Would people compare it to* Genesis? *Would they hate it or like it or . . . or . . . or . . .*

Then came 2020, and our worlds went on a whirlwind ride with loops, curves, drastic drops, and ultimate highs.

And 2021 barreled in like a blur, and still no novel. I needed to prove to myself that I *could* write another book. For me. For you. For us.

After many false starts, my agent, Brenda Bowen, was there to remind me that "the second book is always the hardest." Thank you, Brenda, for allowing me a safe space to be vulnerable enough to admit my fears and brave enough to confront them.

My editor, Caitlyn Dlouhy, never once rushed me for a follow-up book. The pressure I created for myself was already heavy enough. Thank you, Caitlyn, for offering me the gift of time to work through my angst, and for supporting my hand as I explored the genre of verse.

During these last few years, as I pecked out drafts, I

watched my daughter take bold risks. I was impressed, proud, and in awe. Nailah, my dear, you inspire me. Thank you for being you. You give me courage to be me and to bet on myself. And you . . . Remember to bet on yourself. Always.

And while my eyes were on my daughter, my mother's, Phyllis's, eyes were on me. Thank you, Mom, for the reminders that our ancestors watch over me. I strive to make them and you proud.

While waiting on another novel, my mother acted as CEO of my sales team, ensuring every bookstore within her zip code had my books. And most times she's had a partner, my aunt Sandra (Kay). Thank you, Aunt Kay, for sharing this journey with me.

Speaking of teams, I have the *dopest* A-Team who have not only supported me but are simply amazing friends. Love you, Nadia Salem, Candice Calloway, Maria Blackburn, and Robin Green.

While creating this story, I shared bits and pieces with my peers. Thank you, Daria Peoples, Robin Yardi, Victoria Joe, Brittany Janee Thurman, Olugbemisola Rhuday-Perkovich, Mike Jung, Leah Henderson, and Lisa Moore Ramée for our check-ins, venting, encouraging, and sharing of creative energy.

To the unsung heroes, my copy editors, Jeannie Ng and Colleen Fellingham, thank you for your encyclopedia-dictionary-fact-checking expertise. I am in awe of what you do.

And a loud clap and cheer to my Simon & Schuster team. There is so much work behind the scenes, and I appreciate the care that you have given me and this story. Please know I am truly grateful for all of you: Justin Chanda, Michelle Leo, Amy Beaudoin, Morgan Maple, Emily Varga, Caleigh Flegg, Nicole Benevento, Miloni Vora, Deb Sfetsios-Conover, Erin Toller, Chrissy Noh, Lisa Moraleda, and Elizabeth Blake-Linn.

Thank you, Daniel Egnéus, for a beautiful cover, and Danica Novgorodoff, for the lively illustrations.

My dear readers, I reserve the most special thanks for you. You have embraced me and my stories from the very beginning. This is not just my success. This is *our* success.

Each encouraging word, each show of support, is a feather you've given me to add to my wings, so that I may fly.

Each poem, each stanza, each word in *Mid Air* are feathers that I return to you, so that you may fly.

And now, my friends, let us soar together!

MAY - - 2024

Lancaster County Library
313 S White St
Lancaster, SC 29720